GOTHIC NOVELS

GOTHIC NOVELS

Advisory Editor:
Dr. Sir Devendra P. Varma

CONFESSIONS

OF THE NUN

OF ST. OMER

A TALE

Volume 1

ROSA MATILDA

Introduction by Devendra P. Varma

ARNO PRESS

A New York Times Company
in cooperation with
McGRATH PUBLISHING COMPANY
New York—1972

131052

Reprint Edition 1972 by Arno Press Inc.

Special Contents Copyright © 1972 by Devendra P. Varma

LC# 76-131314
ISBN 0-405-00803-1

Gothic Novels
ISBN for complete set: 0-405-00800-7
See last page of this volume for titles.

Manufactured in the United States of America

Introduction

Remarking on this novelist, Montague Summers had said: "There are but few, if any, writers in English fiction whose works are more difficult to discover than are the romances of Charlotte Dacre, better known by the name of Rosa Matilda." With the exception of great Mrs. Radcliffe and Monk Lewis, perhaps there has not been another popular writer of the gothic school than Charlotte Dacre. Born in 1782, she was more famed under her romantic pen name "Rosa Matilda." In her day she was a figure of some celebrity in the literary world. An avowed admirer and disciple of "Monk" Lewis she penned her novels in the style of the first edition of *The Monk*. She wrote novels with piquant titles like *The Libertine* (1807), *The Passions* (1811), and *Confessions of the Nun of St. Omer* (1805), which is dedicated to Lewis himself in admiring terms.

Her *Zofloya* (1806), had "quite enraptured" Shelley and was clearly the source of his two blue-fire romances. According to Summers *Zofloya* is a "first rate gothic romance." "Yet this book is so excessively rare," writes Summers, "that although I have for more than thirty years been minute in my enquiries and indefatigable in my search I have only been able to see two copies."

The influence of *The Monk* upon *Zofloya* is extremely marked. Not only incidents, but even occasionally dialogue and description are reproduced with an almost startling fidelity. The theme of demoniac temptation finds its highest expression in Mephistopheles, the most insidious agent of the philosophy of evil—the same that had tempted *The Monk*, appeared in *Zofloya*. This rare gothic novel has an "enraptured fleshiness" of style and there are incidents of hypnotism, telepathy and satanic chemistry. The popularity of *Zofloya* proved so great that it was soon compressed, nay skeletonised to the compass of a chap-book of a couple of dozen pages, published on August 4, 1810 by Thomas Tegg of 3, Cheapside as *The Daemon of Venice* "An Original Romance by A Lady."

The Libertine is a story based on incest theme and titles of *The Passions* and *Confessions of the Nun of St. Omer* speak for themselves. *The Libertine* achieved a popularity almost equal to *Zofloya*, and it narrates a powerful and distressing story. It was translated into French by Elizabeth de Bon. In *Confessions of the Nun of St. Omer* the incidents and adventures are both melodramatic and intricate, and in spite of crudities and even absurdities, there are striking, forceful passages.

An account of Charlotte Dacre and her writings is contained in *Essays in Petto* (1928) by Montague Summers.

Dalhousie University   *Devendra P. Varma*

CONFESSIONS

OF

THE NUN OF ST. OMER.

A TALE,

IN THREE VOLUMES.

BY

ROSA MATILDA,

VOLUME I.

Virtue is arbitrary, nor admits debate.
To doubt, is treafon in her rigid court.
But if we parly with the foe
We're loft.   G. LILLO.
———————— How many fhake
With all the fiercer tortures of the mind—
Unbounded paffion, madnefs, guilt, remorfe!
                                               THOMSON.

LONDON:

Printed by D. N. SHURY, No. 7, Berwick Street, Soho;
FOR J. F. HUGHES, WIGMORE STREET,
CAVENDISH SQUARE.

1805.

M. G. LEWIS, ESQ.

———

Sir,

Allow me to dedicate to you the following pages, written at eighteen; not from any similarity they can boast to the style or subject of your writings, but simply as a slight tribute for the pleasure I have experienced in perusing them, and the admiration I entertain for your very various and brilliant talents.

I have the honor to be, Sir,
    Your humble servant,
       ROSA MATILDA.

APOSTROPHE

TO

THE CRITICS.

———

'TIS unwillingly I emerge from fe-
ifion to launch my bark on the broad
clean of the world, and battle againſt
oce tide of public opinion; for I write
thom the feelings of the heart. I have
frot culled my phrafes, nor fought to
neck this narrative in the poetic flowers
de eloquence.—I confefs I ftand in awe
of the critics, for I am diffident of my-

self—I fear they will lafh the effervefcence of its fentiments, and the enthufiafm of its fancy; but let them remember, I write not to *palliate* either,
but to exemplify their fatal tendency.

Good Critics, I am young, therefore
folicit your forbearance; revife, com-
pare, and analyfe if you will, but let
your ftrictures be liberal and confide-
rate.

ROSA MATILDA.

INTRODUCTION.

THE following pages, and the Apoſtrophe to the Critics which precedes them, were written at the age of eighteen, chiefly as a reſource againſt *ennui* and for want of better employment: ſoon after they were finiſhed, I had occaſion to leave this country, and I conſigned them, along with ſome other papers, to a box till I returned.

They remained unnoticed for nearly three years, when ſhewing, ſome weeks ſince, ſeveral of my more recent productions to a friend, a few looſe pages

of this tale accidentally caught his eye;
he requeſted permiſſion to peruſe it entire—this I granted, and the reſult of
his arguments, after peruſal, were ſuch
as to induce its preſent publication.

I mention theſe circumſtances from a
conviction, that much, which will now un-
dergo the ordeal of critical examinatio"
requires conſiderable palliation; whether or not ſuch palliation as I have
been enabled to offer may diſarm ſe-
vere ſcrutiny, I am not competent to
aſcertain; but this I feel, if it will not,
to add more would be ſuperfluous.

THE AUTHOR.

CONFESSIONS

OF

THE NUN OF ST. OMER.

CHAP. I.

THE FATAL ENCOUNTER.

DREADFUL conflict!—whether to acknowledge to a son, who reveres me, the melancholy errors of an unfortunate mother, or by suffering him to remain in ignorance of those sad truths it is my

duty

duty to inform him of, retain, only by
an effort of duplicity, his unmerited re-
fpect and love!

And wilt thou then, dear boy—wilt
thou indeed defpife me?—if thou doft,
thou art unlike St. Elmer. Wilt thou not
draw a veil over my errors, and in lieu
of keen contempt gaze on my grave
with pity?—Yes, thou fhalt know all,
my Lindorf; and may it teach thee to
confider, from the forrows of thy parent,
her unhappy fex as defencelefs; and
thus deriving a *dearer* claim on thy
protection, rather than from the eminence of manhood, view them as the
ready - formed victims for deceit and
cruelty. Yes, though at the rifk of
lofing the only joy that is left me, thy
affection

affection and respect, dear son of tears,
I will make atonement (if such there can
be) for my guilt, by inflicting on my
lacerated heart the pain of unequivocal
confession, and remembering that he who
will peruse it is my only friend, the only
being whose love I am desirous to retain.
When I have surmounted the melancholy
struggle, a ray of peace may faintly gild
my bosom * * * * the severest
philosophy and the conflicts of my whole
life can extort no more than this—Lindorf, I will lay open to thy knowledge
my agonizing tale * * * * * *
* * * * * * * * * * *

Should the inclosed packet, as I trust,
come sacred to the hands of Dorvil Lindorf, let him not, as he respects the memory of an ill-fated mother, peruse it

B 4   till

till the cold and friendly grave hath damped for ever the warm flushed cheek of shame. * * * * * * * *
* * * * * * * * * * * *
* * * * My father was the Marquis Arieni;—making the tour of Europe, he became acquainted with an English family of diſtinction reſiding in England; and, probably imagining he beheld in my mother the woman he had ever deſired as a wife, he made propoſals to her parents, which were accepted, and they became united.

Arieni was an haughty Italian—daring, a great ſpeculator, fond of pre-eminence and of ſtrong abilities;—his perſon was ſhort, yet graceful—and his manners, though reſerved, inſidious—

a ſpirit

a spirit of enterprise and shrewdness of imagination calculated him for the atchievement of events the most hazardous; and an eloquential flow of language, dazzling and sententious, made to him continual converts of the weak and wise.

My mother was his enthusiastic admirer——she contemplated his talents with the same awe-struck wonder as a child views the ascension of a sky-rocket:——she was innocent, young, and romantic to a fault, easily swayed, and too soft to be energetic, or repel by dignified perseverance the influx of oppression.

After their marriage my parents launched into a splendour beyond their

power

power to continue—eight years rolled
on amid the vortex of folly, but at the
expiration of that period, the embarraff-
ments of the Marquis would fuffer him
no longer to remain with fafety in the
metropolis, and yielding to the fuggeftions of his friends he confented to fly,
caufing me to accompany him, who
had ever been his favorite—unfortunate
child! on whofe innocent head Fate had
already fet her gloomy mark.

Now left wretched and forlorn with
two children younger than myfelf, my
mother retired into an obfcure village—
there, her heart breaking with defpondency, fhe paffed her hours in tears, in
praying for her hufband, in dreaming
over his image, and in inftructing her
children.   For

For me, wild and carelefs as the breeze which wafted over me, I little dreamt the forrows of my parents; and with the childifh art of eight years endeavoured to awaken the attention of the Marquis.

Italy was the place of deftination—fome connexions he had there, with, perhaps, an involuntary defire to revifit his native country, had confpired in his choice of an abode.—We arrived after a long and fatiguing journey, when my father, defirous of refting as early as poffible, alighted at the firft Locanda (an inn) which prefented itfelf—he was informed the apartments were all occupied either by families or individuals.

" But could you not prevail on *any*

individual,

individual, friend ?" inquired my father with an expreffive fmile, and accompanying the fmile by a *more* expreffive donation.

" There is one apartment, Sinor, the beft we have, in the poffeffion of only *one* lady, but fhe is a lady of rank, Sinor, and perhaps might object."

" Go, friend, and ufe your influence ; if you fucceed—you underftand me"— and again my father fmiled ; the man bowed .obfequioufly and withdrew on his embaffy—in about five minutes he returned.

" The Sinora gives confent, Sinor," exclaimed the enraptured mercury.

" Lead

" Lead on then," said my father, alighting and taking me in his arms.

We were ushered into a superb apartment, where a lady of elegant figure and shewy appearance had been evidently studying an attitude against our entrance, and now half rose from the sopha, on which, nymph-like, she reclined; the Marquis appeared struck, yet in a graceful manner apologized for his intrusion, and half hesitating, half presuming, seated himself near the reclining nymph.

They entered into conversation—sad and diabolical woman !——infamous source of all my errors and my woes ! why did no kind presage no instinctive
emotion

emotion inform me of the forrows thou waſt fated to heap upon me?—playfully I hung around the ſyren ſmiler, and ſportively amuſed myſelf with her reſplendent ornaments.

The Counteſs Roſendorf was a German of noble extraction; but high birth, which might have reflected additional luſtre on her virtues, ſeemed only tarniſhed by her crimes: one *exalted* vicious character, from whom the multitude take lead, is of more momentous danger to ſociety then twenty of a *common* caſt. She had been married in her youth to a man ſhe could little appreciate, whoſe miſplaced affection not allowing him to reſent her infamous conduct, but whoſe heart incapable of ſupporting

porting it, *burſt* beneath the variety of wretchedneſs ſhe inflicted. and left her to purſue alone a life which had already become tainted with every vice.——She had two children, *ſuppoſed* to be Count Roſendorf's; for ſeveral years after his death her conduct had given riſe to various reports, as in its fulleſt extent ſhe. followed the motto of *liverty*, literally ſhunned and diſdained by the noble family ſhe had diſgraced.

She was artful, vivacious, and elegant —of an enterpriſing and atrocious ſpirit —a depraved heart, ſalacious diſpoſition, and inſenſible ſoul;——ſhe appeared to have determined the ſubjugation of my father; *he* appeared worthy of the taſk— her fortune, from the uncircumſcribed courſe

courſe ſhe had purſued, was more than
ſhattered; but her *ſpirit* ſtill remained
unbroken, and ſhe preſumed to hope
that his notions of independence accorded with her own. From this *fateful*
period my doom aſſumed its caſt ; 'twas
of gloomy black—*my* doom was aſcer-
tained, that of my unfortunate family,
and, perhaps, it might have affected
the future fate of myriads yet unborn :
for have not the revolutions of empires
depended on the influence of the moment, and the long chain of events
which, ſtill hidden in embryo, taken from
it their ſubſequent caſts * * * *
* * * * * * * * * * * *
* * * * * let me not dwell upon
the maddening theme, but haſten on.—
Fate now ſmiled gloomy upon my
blaſted

blaſted days—a deſtructive and illicit
union was gradually cemented between
my father and the Roſendorf; and the
fragment of a letter which I accidentally
diſcovered, and by chance preſerved,
ſufficiently evinces the unbluſhing tur-
pitude of this female ſeducer.—It ran
thus:

"Arieni, you are a man to whom
the prejudices of the world are as
nothing; I confeſs, from the ideas I had
conceived of you, I had not imagined
this advance on my ſide would have
been neceſſary. Arieni appeared to
me to act from himſelf, not from others;—
is your mind big with any project, and
do you fear to avow it?—Are not you
and I above the *common* kind; have we
not

not each been moſt prepoſterouſly miſ-
matched by the idle prevalence of a
political inſtitution?—our *minds* are
congenial and *ought* to be united;—of
what conſequence ſhould be to us the
world's opinion?—you are ruined, and
will they affiſt you?—Of what cohſe-
quence the ties of prejudice—reaſon and
right evidently point out to man the
path of happineſs:—he is a fool—no
philoſopher, if he purſue it not.

My motto is *liberty* and independance!
Arieni has called me dangerous, but
wherefore if I convince him I am *juſt?*
—if not, how can I be dangerous?—
You tell me of your wife—fallacious
obſtacle!--truſt to her *affection* for *pardon,*
to her *reaſon* for *toleration;* if ſhe love
you

you as you fay, fhe can never feek *re-venge*—for her tendernefs will yield to the arguments you will know fo well how to adduce ; if fhe prove refractory fhe has then *no* affection, and we are juftified in peremptorily retaining our free agency : *remember,* that our fortunes are *fhattered;* that together we may reftore them, and that fhe who offers you her friendfhip and her perfon, is poffeft at once of fpirit to *conceive* and promptnefs to *execute.*"

Was my young heart inftructed then in the fateful net, weaving forever againft its future happinefs ?—I know not, but I viewed the Rofendorf with *increafing* terror and diflike. A fuperb palace was hired in the heart of the
Campania

Campania de Roma, and whatever were the fpeculations of ambition, for which fo much had been facrificed, they were by no means aerial. The palace Arieni became rapidly crouded with the firft nobility of Italy, and feftive mirth appeared to reign throughout.

CHAP. II.

JUVENILE ATTACHMENTS.

AMONG the various influx of fociety that vifited the palace of the Marquis, was a young Englifh Nobleman,
called St. Elmer, dear and unfortunate
being, whofe lot was fo deeply tinctured
with the fatality of mine! St. Elmer
was of the firft order of human beings;
his character was too *fine* for delineation;
all that was generous, all that was fincere

cere and noble : of virtue the moft refined—of fentiments divine—philanthropic—oh! how much infpired by that
lovely enthufiafm which elevates, not
maddens, the heart in which it dwells.

His countenance was a touching index
of his pure and heavenly mind; his
large blue eyes contained an expreffion
of voluptuous fentiment almoft too fine
to look upon, yet would a caft of mild
feverity pafs fometimes over his fafcinating features;—the tint of his com-
plexion, without brilliancy, was fuch as
at once to intereft the *heart*, while the
graceful elegance of his figure, the feductive melody of his voice, and the refinement of his manners, feemed to en-
chant into his favor beings the moft
                              ftubborn

ftubborn and the moft mifanthropical.

Though differing fo widely from Italian chara&ter, he was generally courted;
for me, if I but heard his foft footftep in
the hall, my young heart underwent a
peculiar agitation; I have fince often
dwelt on him with wondering emotion—I
would fly from childifh amufement, from
juvenile affociates, to welcome him, to
hover near him, and attra& his notice.
I would twine my fingers in his auburn
ringlets, and relate to him the occur-
rences of the day ;—with fportive vivacity he would return my innocent ad-
vances, and feem delighted when I
bounded to his arms. Gradually I forgot
my deferted home, and all who apper-
tained

-tained to it; pleafure and St. Elmer employed wholly my ideas.

At this period, I was fcarcely more than eight years of age. Three years more rolled on, and things continued thus fituated, when an affair in which the Marquis had unfortunately engaged together with fome young men of rank, rendered him, in a land of bravos, in momentary danger of his life; he had been involuntarily drawn into the tranf-action at the requeft of fome friends, which not having terminated with the expected eclat, threw a fort of odium, however unmerited, upon all who had been engaged in it. He determined to quit Italy, and the perfevering Rofen-dorf determined to accompany him; both

both agreed as to the policy and propriety of returning into Germany, where the degenerate Countefs *profeſſed* to have connections, who however ſcorned to countenance her.

Preparations were concluded with the utmoſt expedition, and in a paroxyſm of grief bordering on deſpair, *I* was torn from the boſom of St. Elmer.— Was it wonderful that I ſhould *feel* ?—I was now eleven years of age—in a mind, of ſtrong ſuſceptibility the emotions are early matured. I affirm that I *felt* at being torn from St. Elmer, and even at this moment I can recollect, with a keenneſs of ſenſation almoſt incedible, the exceſs of ſadneſs I then experienced.— St. Elmer was a man, and yet *he* wept !

more than one warm tear fell into my bofom; and my ftrong agony communicated to his fufceptible bofom an emotion which was fufficiently apparent.

" Dear Cazire," he faid in a melodious accent, " my dear little girl, we fhall meet again."

" Oh! never, never!" I fobbed with emphatic earneftnefs.

" But indeed we *fhall*," he replied, preffing me in his arms, and gazing on me with a tearful eye—

" Begone, Cazire," cried the Countefs: " my Lord St. Elmer, forgive the child!" " Pardon

" Pardon her rudenefs," added the
Marquis.

Oh ! cruel perverfion ! are then the
fineft emotions of the heart fo ill appre-
ciated as to be ftyled rude?

" Dear girl," cried St. Elmer, " I
wifh fhe was not going;" and looked
expreffively at my father.

" And would your Lordfhip be *troubled*
with the imp ?" inquired the Rofendorf.

" Oh! might I be permitted to retain her," anfwered St. Elmer, as he
viewed my ftarting tears, momentarily
arrefted by the fuggeftions of hope.

My

My father laughed; " You are wild,"
he cried, " St. Elmer, in your requeſt;
but I could as ſoon reſign my life, as
that child!—ſhe has been for eleven
years my chiefeſt joy, and, in all my various ſorrows and diſappointments, my
only conſolation."

" And far be it from *me*," returned
St. Elmer, " to intrude upon the ſacred
affection of a father for his child; but
you muſt leave me, love—you muſt indeed!—theſe warm tears unman me
quite." He ſeated himſelf on the ſopha,
and as the Marquis approached to take
me from his arms, I clung round his
neck with renovated anguiſh.

But,

But, alas! what could *my* ſtruggles
avail?—I was conſigned to the care of
a ſervant, my young heart agonized
with the violence of my ſorrow.

CHAP. III.

RETROSPECTION.

I WENT to bed weeping and unhappy. In the morning, on awaking, I found a little medallion set in diamonds, with the cypher of St. Elmer in his hair, suspended from my neck by a black ribbon.

" And how came I by this?" I inquired of Jean my servant.

" My Lord St. Elmer, as you slept——"

" And why was I not awakened?" I pettishly demanded.

" My

" My Lord would not permit."

How did this incident imprefs my mind! how did it flatter the little vanity of my bofom! I rofe fomewhat happier; we were to depart immediately, and commence our journey. My father was thoughtful and referved; the Rofendorf amufed herfelf with an Italian grey-hound; and I meditated on my dear medallion.

Sweet and noble country! what a mine of ideas muft thy fublimely beautiful profpects excite in a reflective mind! with how much rapture muft it dwell upon thy glowing imagery of various nature, on thy trembling moun-

tains,

tains, feeming fufpended between fea and air, on flaming Vefuvius majeftically dreadful, on the afpiring Alps! to gaze upon the diftant heavens feeming near, or on the varying fhades tinting the ridgy rocks! to hang over the narrow point of a precipice, and dwell with luxuriant horror from its dizzying height upon the dangerous depths below!

And then, the gay Carvinal—not to mix in its diffipated crouds I long, but from far to watch with pleafing fadnefs the joys, the filly amufements-I fhall never more partake—to hear from a diftant cafement the tempered note ftealing foft over the ripling wave—to hearken with fad emotion to the diftant hum of men—the carelefs jocund laugh breaking
on

on the ſtillneſs of the night—the ſplaſhing
of the oars—the gradually ſinking cadence
of the whining ſong—the lights now ſeen
miſtily, now ſhining at intervals through
various breaks—the crouds—the thought-
leſs myriads of mortal men laughing and
fighting among each other like ſo many
children in a garden—the tricked-out
gondolas ſailing merrily along, and the
ſoft ſounds of the ſerinaders aſcending
in aerial ſtrains, awaking the melancholy
heart to emotions various as indeſcrib-
able !

But whither am I wandering? again
in the fairy labyrinths of fancy?—in the
wilds of Imagination?—oh! dear and
dangerous power, why do I ſtill indulge
in *thee* ?—haſt thou not yet withdrawn

thy

thy ruinous spell from my shattered
heart?—who hears?—who listens?—
Cazire, art thou not an inmate of St.
Omer?—who hears thee, then, within the
dreary convent walls?—Hark to the
solemn midnight chaunt! Hark! now
it swells—away with worldly feelings—
away too with emotions of the heart—
the gloom of superstition owns them
not!

CHAP. IV.

CLOUDS STILL GATHER.

MY dear Lindorf, my laſt was in a melancholy ſtrain : I will endeavour, if poſſible, to check in future the perſonalities of grief.

A variety of objects cannot fail of amuſing a youthful mind yet untinctured by evil, and a few days after my arrival in Germany, I regained my uſual vivacity.

We proceeded to a ſeat of the Roſendorf's, who propoſed to my father that

c 6   the

the young Ellenburgh, her daughter,
fhould be taken from the convent, where
from her earlieft childhood fhe had been
placed, and then, by introducing her to
the world of fafhion, fpeculate upon a
marriage with fome fool of fortune. My
father did not object to this motion, and
her fon, who was at an academy near the
convent of Ellenburgh, was to accompany his fifter home ; this plan was foon
executed. I was amufing myfelf in the
garden which furrounded the houfe,
when the young ftrangers alighted ; in-
ftinctively my heart fell, and I followed
them up ftairs with looks of *dire* defpondency.

" What has happened ?" inquired my
father as I entered. I flew towards him,
and clafping my hands around his neck,
I exclaimed with agony of grief, point-

ing to Ellenburgh and her brother,
"Alas! I fhall now be deprived for ever
of your love!"

" Silly girl," replied my father, preffing me in his arms, as though he did it
by ftealth; " why fhould you think fo?"

" St. Elmer is not here—I have no
friend but *you*."

" I think the little girl is very rude,"
faid Ellenburgh, going to the glafs.

" And fo think I," added her brother
Donamar, feizing his fifter round the
neck, and giving her a kifs.

My tears redoubled!

"And what now?" inquired my father.

" I have no brother nor sister to kiss me."

" But do not *I* love you, Cazire ?"

" But *you* will not love me always, my dear father."

" How can you humor that capricious girl, Arieni ?" said the Rosendorf; " I assure you it's vastly ridiculous."

" Forbear a word on the subject," said my father ; " dear child ! my heart would break if she were miserable."

" And ah! my father, what crime did I commit when I was thrust an exile from your arms ?—had you but ever loved

loved me thus—thus ever have *afferted* your love, never, never would your unfortunate Cazire have been facrificed to deftruction! I had never feen Arieni fo much affected; I felt his kindnefs, for I felt deferted; but to me, expreffions of his affection were no novelty; with me he was all doting fondnefs, indulgent tendernefs, and affability; with others, haughty, faftidious, and referved. I feemed to conftitute his chief delight, and I adored *him* with unbounded enthufiafm.

By degrees, however, I became familiarifed to the young ftrangers; we did not regard each other with fuch inquiring jealoufy, and appeared inclined to amity. Ellenburgh was about fifteen,

vain

vain and affected, though with some
share of natural beauty, intended to be
heightened by a recourse to arts which
had a contrary effect; and her childish
figure, decked absurdly in the habili-
ments of the woman, formed an appearance displeasing and grotesque. Of her
mind I can observe little; it was one
of those we see every day clasped in
the unaspiring rank of non-entities;
she had no will but her mother's, and no
wish to have a will of her own.

Her brother Donamar was a tall half-
formed boy, with a shrill irregular voice;
he was noisy, presumptuous, and tyranni-
cal; his countenance fair, with large
grey eyes, but vacant; and for his
mind, it might rank with his sister's,
claiming

claiming the addition only of exceffive arrogance.

However inclined I might have been to view the faireft fide of the picture, I foon perceived my fituation became irkfome and unhappy. I was neglected and impofed on, without power to explain myfelf; and faw with increafing anguifh the mind of my father biaffed againft me, and his cherifhed affections gradually diminifh. In folitude I pined and wept the commencement of my forrows! The following inftance which occurred, perhaps, accelerated the alienation of my father's heart; and, though trifling, may elucidate the unhappinefs of my fituation.

We

We were all three playing one evening in a long gallery leading from various apartments to the fitting room, then occupied by my father and the Countefs;—Donamar, ever boifterous in his mirth, pufhed me fo forcibly againft his fifter ftanding near the door of the apartment, that it burft open, and fhe fell forwards to the utter confternation of her mother, who immediately rifing and perceiving me only near, (for Donamar had made his efcape,) revenged on me her daughter's fall, with a blow which brought the tears into my eyes. To fee me perfonally injured, even yet my father could not hear, and rifing with indignation, he repaid the infult on the late exulting check of Ellenburgh. This occafioned

a battle

a battle between the parents of each;
when my father, eager to save *me* from
further ill treatment, thruſt me up a
couple of ſteps into an adjoining chamber, and locked me in. High words and
bitter language then enſued, and I heard
at intervals the trembling voice of Ellenburgh diſſuading the opponents from
their fray; ſtill it continued, and they
parted at length mutually enraged.

Thus it may eaſily be perceived, that
however the compact of *intereſts* may
agree, the union of *hearts* muſt be effected on a nobler baſis.

Alas! the affection of the Marquis, temporarily rouſed by my injuries, ſtill de-
creaſed: when he reflected on the diſ-
agreeable

agreeable reproaches it had expofed him
to, he looked on me as the caufe, however innocent, of his breach with the
Rofendorf; and fhe viewed me with a
fiend-like hatred, as the inftigator of
her impolitic language towards my father, whofe affection, or at leaft good-
will, fhe had an intereft in preferving.

CHAP. VI.

DANGERS OF FALSE SENTIMENT.

YOUNG as I was, obfervation convinced me I fhould not long remain in my prefent fituation, and a converfation between my father and the Rofendorf (which, as it refpected myfelf, I made no fcruple of endeavouring from an adjoining room to overhear) confirmed me in my melancholy fufpicions.

" Arieni,"

" Arieni," faid the Countefs, " our
quarrels methinks have of late become *frequent.* I remember with regret the time when haimony reigned
for ever."

" And why do we quarrel, Rofendorf ?"

" There *is* a caufe, which, though
apparently trifling, is the *only* one,
and imprudently difregarded."

" What mean you ?"

" That Cazire, (it pains me to fay,)
for a girl of her age, is capable of art
moft exceffive, and adds to it a mali-
cious tongue; which, if either of
my

my own children unfortunately were curſed with, they ſhould not dwell an hour under the SAME *roof with me !"*

" You are *prejudiced* againſt that child, ſhe is 'too young to be artful; but I do not expect your affection for *her*—ſhe is not *your* child."

" I am not ſo illiberal, Arieni—let us compromiſe; remove Cazire for a *ſhort time;* and if every diſagreement, quarrel, or unpleaſant diſturbance ceaſe not from her departure, I will not only agree to facilitate her return, but bring her back myſelf, and acknowledge my error."

" You

" You muſt not expeᓴ *me* to agree immediately to a propoſal of this nature; I will have ſome converſation with her, watch her conduᓴ, and try her ſome time longer; if ſhe prove incorrigible, I will place her in a convent."

The Counteſs urged no further, and the ſubjeᓴ changed. But from this luckleſs hour, as the Roſendorf had made an opening, ſhe never ceaſed till her deſire was obtained; in vain was, on *my* ſide, conduᓴ the more irreproachable—in vain did I *bear* and *forbear*—in vain endure all that malice could ſuggeſt, or the moſt. determined cruelty invent; I ſaw with ſorrow, ſaw my de parture draw nearer every day.

Mean-

Meantime the letters of my mother increafed in defpondency;—fhe begged, fhe fupplicated of my father to return; —fhe offered to work, to ftarve, to die for him! little confcjous of the influence he was enjoying—little confcious of the fad events which had taken place; and, laftly, fhe talked of joining him if he did not fpeedily revifit England. This laft infinuation roufed the Marquis as from a dream of torpor; he faw it became neceffary to account for an abfence, lengthened already beyond the bounds of equivocal palliations, and determined on revealing as cautioufly as poffible what could not for ever remain concealed. In what language he explained to her the ftep he had taken, or how he prevailed on her to tolerate it,

VOL. I.   D   I know

I know not, but he permitted her to visit Germany, and bought for her a beautiful and romantic cottage in the village of Staub. Her anſwer pourtrays ſufficiently the idolatrous love ſhe bore my father and the romantic quixotiſm of her nature; ſhews too, that falſe ſentiment and chimerical notions of magnanimity are the moſt fatal rocks for a mind, unaided by the ſtronger powers of energetic reaſon, to encounter.

" Cruel Arieni! think you not I could have diſpenſed with ſo dreadful, ſo deſperate a proof of your affeâion?—your letter of horrors lies before me, and my ſtreaming eyes glare on it confuſedly, ſcarcely able to *credit* the contents. I ſeem to view as a long illuſive dream the

laſt

laft five years of my exiftence; from which, on awaking, I find myfelf oppreffed by *real* accumulated horrors, and chief of the gloomy proceffion is the defertion of Arieni. Was it then to *fave* me?—to *fave* your innocent family from ruin, that you ftabbed me with your abfence to the heart, and *now* only draw forth the barbed arrow to plunge it deeper in?—why did you recover me from a five years' delufion to fend me *mad* at laft? oh! why, I afk, was this cruel proof *neceffary?*—together we could have conjeftured a thoufand plans; *fome* could not have failed; but feparated, torn afunder like the ivy from the oak! the oak may flourifh; flourifh *long* 'tis true, but the *devoted ivy* already feeks the earth.

D 2   " *Forgive*

" *Forgive* you, Arieni—alas! I muſt —did real love ever ſeek *revenge?* you ſhall not find me your inferior in the affection you profeſs; and if *you* had magnanimity enough to become a ſacrifice, I have magnanimity enough to water that ſacrifice with my tears! but I have not magnanimity to *ſmile* on it. Alas. how dreadful it is for *love* to increaſe and *hope* to decay! for, Arieni, we are ſeparated, and I am *determined,* ſince you dare not be mine from *choice,* you *never* ſhall from *coercion. Will* I come? you aſk—alas! how many have underſtanding enough to *condemn* thoſe actions they have not *fortitude* to *reſiſt;* and come I *muſt,* though all the powers of *reaſon* battled againſt it.

    " A M E L I A   A R I E N I."

What

What could be more indicative of a romantic mind, but of naturally good *principles*, than this letter! Had my miftaken mother, in lieu of liftening to the mad dictates of *imaginary* enthufiafm, attended to its milder opponent *reafon*, and been fwayed by common fenfe, how much mifery might have been avoided! The torrent of *falfe* fentiment, the *pomp* of *found*, which. lure fo many to deftruction, bore down all before it ; and a delufive attachment, poffeffing for its bafis a fomething *fatal* which cannot be defcribed (for it was evidently neither *reafon* nor *virtue* tended to *accelerate* the melancholy frenzy,) while the fubtle influence of my father, *impofing* on the dangerous weaknefs he fhould have *pitied*, fealed *for ever* the fad fiat of my future misfortunes.

Never

Never fhould the fuggeftions of wild infidious *fancy* preponderate againft *real good*, or the defire of appearing vainly enthufiaftic, militate againft virtue or happinefs. It is not ourfelves alone we injure, by the felfifh fallacy; for *no* human being, unlefs ifolated from the *world*, can be *fingly* unfortunate by his own folly : we are all invifibly linked, and the fall of *one* includes the fall of *many*. We may effect by one falfe ftep the fate of myriads *unborn*, and render ourfelves unaccountable for the vices and follies unmerited calamity may entail upon them, by the irrefiftible confluence of events.

CHAP. VI.

THE EXILE.

AT length an anſwer, wrung from me in the bitterneſs of my heart towards the rancorous Roſendorf for ſome unmerited reproach, which my proud boſom ſwelled to ſuffer, accelerated at once the ſtorm which had long been gathering, and ſent me an exile from the boſom of my father. It was determined to place me for a year or two,

at

at leaſt, in ſome elegant convent for the occaſional reception of boarders, and ſometimes, though ſeldom, to ſuffer my viſits to the fancied Eden, from which I had ſo cruelly been driven.

Meantime my mother having ſigni-fied her conſent to the propoſition of my father, he procured for her a romantic cottage, ſuch as he knew would indulge the effervefcence of her brain, where ſhe might live iſolated and penſive, in a bower of rural ſweets, imaginarily happy in the innocence of her conduct, and careleſs alike of the low opprobrium or vulgar pity of an inſenſible world. *This* was to make amends to her for the in-jury ſhe had ſuſtained, and ſooth her fancy while her happineſs was betrayed.

Here

Here it was likewife intended I fhould
fometimes vifit her; and when the period
for my ftay at the convent fhould be
completed, take up with her my continued refidence.

Notwithftanding the unhappinefs of my
fituation, the unkind treatment I had
experienced from the Rofendorf and her
children, I ftill felt (independant of the
pain I experienced at quitting my father) an emotion of regret almoft to
agony; for the heart muft be ftrangely
infenfible that can *quit* with tearlefs eye
early affociations, almoft *endeared* from
habit and places, which acquire a fort
of *magic* charm, merely becaufe they
vill be feen *no more*; for fuch prefen-
timent affailed *me* at the time of departure.

ture. The Countefs too was more kind
than I had ever known her; but too art-
lefs to inveftigate motives, I faw not ill-
concealed joy beneath the treacherous
fmile which marked her features, and
fancied the fame affection infpired *her*
as this moment I felt ftruggling in my
own bofom. I forgot her paft treatment, and wept with unaffected forrow.

My father placed me in the carriage;
a female fervant attended me to the
convent, and my eyes blinded by tears,
my heart heaving with unexpreffed forrow, I was driven a melancholy exile
from his fight.

Towards the fall of evening we arrived on the borders of a beautiful fo-
reft;

reſt; an edifice of majeſtic and exquiſite
ſtructure attracted my ſight: " Oh !" I
exclaimed to my companion, " if that
were but the Convent."

" That *is* the Convent of St. Omer,"
anſwered Jean.

We continued drawing near—a ſtrain
of melodious harmony roſe on the ſul-
len air; the ſolemn organ ſent forth
its melancholy ſound, and a tone of
celeſtial ſoftneſs, that ſeemed calculated
to *ſearch* the *ſoul*, firſt ſtole gently on the
boſom of the ſwelling gale; till, gradually riſing to the full chorus of harmony,
it ſunk again imperceptibly upon the
raviſhed ear in a ſlow declining chaunt,
leaving the mind open to the moſt

lively

lively impreffions of delightful fadnefs, and ftill reverberating in the *fancied choir* of imagination. At length we reached the feducive habitation, where the mifery of the moment, feeking to be ameliorated, is entailed for ever; whence the unfortunate victim, *mifantrophifed* by long and repented feclufion, endeavours with luring colors to attract the unweary fool who fports without. Thus a decoyed fongfter of the woods, enclofed within a wiry cage, feeks to entrap its heedlefs fellow to a fimilar fate. *This* is the adverfity which hardens the heart. To be *compelled* to mourn when the heart would reanimate; to be *forced* into horrors and ifolation! *this* gives not to the foul the penfive *philanthropic* forrow fo fallacioufly depicted; it fteels the heart

to

to every foft impreffion, and bids us deftroy the liberty we can no longer
enjoy.

We entered the Convent, and as I
waited in the parlour for the abbefs, a
number of boarders crouded round me,
and appeared rejoiced in the acquifition
of a new affociate – In early youth the
impreffions of grief and joy are equally
tranfient ! the emotions of each are the
tear and fmile of a moment : like feathers
borne on the unfteady gale, we are
actuated by each *fucceffive* breath, carelefs and unmindful how or where.

I began to think the monaftery of St.
Omer (although I was compelled thi-
ther) might be a charming place ; and

to

to wifh I had been led by *choice* rather than *coercion;* for the very idea of *that* either funk my heart with defpondency, or fwelled it with indignation: in fhort, I faw Jean depart with comparative eafinefs, and endeavoured to return with gratitude the affiduous attention of my young affociates.

Thus two or three months ftole away pleafantly enough; I was inftructed in various branches of fuperficial education, but reading was my chief delight; dangerous, though charming power, capable alike to improve or to deftroy! Jean, to entertain me, procured fometimes fuch books as fhe could take unperceived from my father's library. Her choice was in general fixed by the title; and

and she purchased for me at my own
desire those which from similar reasons
she supposed most pleasing. These, like
the poisonous poppy, affected my brain
with their dangerous influence, and
dazzled my senses with the vivid strength
of their coloring. Under the fallacious
mask of conveying *virtue* to the heart, the
most subtle and agreeable emotions were
infused; passionate scenes were depicted in all the glowing imagery of
voluptuous language, to shew the
wonderful escapes of innocence: whatever was calculated to inflame the
senses, and enervate the heart to *rational*
pleasures, was drawn with dangerous
fascination. The *seducer* was decked in
all the charms of beauty, *involuntary*
error, but acknowledged principle;—
his

his wanderings thofe of the head merely, not the heart ; and the rofes were thus too thickly ftrewn to difcover the thorns. Inftead of feeling the indignation which thus is deprecated, treacherous emotions of *pity* fteal into the deluded bofom !— love and defire follow : the pretended *guard* and caution become in reality the chief feducers ! the heart is enflaved through the *medium* of the fenfes ; for thefe are *firft* enervated, and, concentrating their feducive powers, call every paffion to their aid. *Thefe* delude the heart, which, drowned in the indefcribable voluptuoufnefs of its own fenfations, falls a ready and refiftlefs martyr.

Mine, warm and fufceptible from nature to a degree of madnefs—every feeling

feeling a paffion, and every paffion a
principle, could not reftrain the feducive torrent which thus poured in upon its
dangerous fentiments. Reflection might
warn, but her voice was loft in the tu-
mult of the paffions; and the dear emotions which accompanied their gradual
accefs to the mind, blinded the very eyes
of *Reafon* with a tear of tranfport.

CHAP. VII.

DANGEROUS READING.

I SHALL pafs over two years of my refidence in the convent of St. Omer, and content myfelf with informing you that my furor for dangerous reading increafed with the injury it did me. Naturally of a difpofition and ideas that required the utmoft *power* of education to check, I was abandoned (at an age when every impreffion, whether deftructive

tive or otherwife, remains fixed on the
heart with unabated ftrength) to my own
guidance; that is, I was inftructed in all
that is neceffary for a *female* to know;
my exterior was polifhed, but that which
required precifely the *greateft* care was
difregarded—my mind was the wildeft
feat of anarchy and error; my imagination wandering uncontrolled in the fairy
regions of fiction and romance, my
heart feduced by its refiftlefs power,
while my reafon feemed like a diftreffed
pilot in a ftorm, effaying in vain to rule
the boifterous gales which threatened its
deftruction.

At fifteen it is in vain to attempt what
was omitted at eleven; the mind cannot
too early be guarded againft the wild
influx

influx of paffion; for in youth *imagina-*
tion is ftrong a..d *reafon* weak; we conceive an idea, it becomes pleafing, we
dwell on it repeatedly, it entwines with
our exiftence, it fafcinates the brain—for
the heart would always bribe the reafon
to a partnerfhip; like a child, fearful it is
on the point of committing fomething
rafh, would inveigle its wifer parent as a
fanction. *Perhaps* this idea may be
fallacious and deftructive, but it has in-
corded with the fibres of the heart, and,
like the treacherous ivy, poifon is in its
grafp. What can now be done? to root
it out is impoffible, or along with it we
muft root out the heart; the evil muft
grow with our growth, and its deftructive
influence fpread around. No fkilful
philanthropift analized *my* young fenfations,

tions, and weeded away when it could
not have been felt the poifonous *show-
plants* that mingled with the flowers,
anxious to arrogate the foil to them-
felves. The mind in infancy is a blank
fheet; a character is impreffed—then
another and another, but in vain; though
a thoufand different impreffions fhould
afterwards be made, the character of the
firft will *still* be afcertained, and influence in a degree the character of every
after-impreffion.

The mind muft be employed—if it
do not good, it will do ill. The monaftery of St. Omer had foon loft its
charms with me, and my imagination,
naturally variable, required fomething
on which to fix its attention. As I read
I dif-

I difcovered with rapture that I had
fprung a mine of inexhauftible delight;
but I foon grew weary of reading the
actions of *others*; I longed myfelf to be
called into energetic exertion, and defpifed the dull, unvaried routine of my
exiftence.

Jean, who loved me, and whofe honeft indignation feemed excited by the
treatment I had experienced, furnifhed
me clandeftinely with volumes as romantic as the moft avaricious fancy could
defire. Here too I trace thy fatal influence, ever barbarous Rofendorf!—by
infpiring honeft hearts with pity at the
fituation thou hadft unneceffarily driven
me to, their well-meaning zeal, undi-
rected by difcernment, turned into fubtle
poifon

poifon that which they intended as balm, tincturing my future exiftence with its deftructive influence.

Some of the books I perufed were more calculated than others to corrupt the underftanding; thefe were moft dangerous; they tolerated the free fentiments they infufed, and fpoke to the fufceptible heart in a language wholly irrefiftible; love was painted happy only when *unfettered*; I felt, as I became enflaved with the brilliancy of the language and fpecioufnefs of the arguments, that they *muft* be juft: thus did my fentiments become more dangerous than ever, for they affumed the garb of reafon.

Sophiftry

Sophiftry (the plaufible incendiary) but clears the way for its pupil Vice. I felt it impoffible to read without loving the author, and deemed it the climax of prejudice to withhold the tribute of unbounded admiration. By degrees my tafte became more felect, a flimfy compofition ftood no chance with me, and I threw it by in difguft; I defired a work wherein I might tread with the vifionary hero or heroine in all the enchanting mazes of love and fentiment, where my native enthufiafm and originality might find ample food; and, in fhort, a work of fpirit, to give frefh zeft to my vitiated tafte, and warm with fires new and various my deluded heart.

CHAP. VIII.

SIXTEEN AND THREE-AND-TWENTY.

DURING my refidence of two years at the convent of St. Omer I had paid a few vifits to my father, which latterly were lefs frequent than ever; fometimes too I faw my mother, who had arrived as early as poffible after the intimation fhe had given, and refided with her children in a beautifully romantic cottage in the village of Staub. From the fhort vifits

I had

I had paid there it was impoſſible I could
form much idea of the family; my mother appeared amiable and unhappy, and
conſequently intereſted a heart ſoftened
beyond the intentions of Nature from
books which had refined ſenſibility to a
pitch of agony; for my ſiſter and my
brother I felt affection and kindneſs.

One morning I was informed, by letter from my father, that he would viſit
me at the Convent, and take me back
with him to dinner, requeſting I would
be ready at the time appointed   I had
not ſeen him for more than two months,
therefore obeyed him with alacrity, and
remained waiting in the parlour for the
diſtant ſound of the carriage round the
walls.   Preſently I heard the rumbling
of

of wheels—the carriage stopped—the door opened—my father entered, accompanied by St. Elmer—yes, it was St. Elmer who accompanied my father.

In an instant I forgot the hypocritical reserve of a romantic heroine, and springing from the chair, threw myself into the expanded arms of my childhood's dear remembered friend.

" Cazire !" cried my father in an angry voice.

" Cazire!" repeated St. Elmer in an emphatic accent.

" *Yes*," I replied, pressing his hand

E 2   to

to my lips with all the *fervor* of a bigot, devoid of his hypocrify.

" Is your *age ftill* eleven?" cried my father with a frown; " your *manners*, I perceive are the fame."

" Oh! be not offended, my father," I replied blufhing; " I am indeed rejoiced to fee St. Elmer."

" Is it poffible?" exclaimed St. Elmer, furveying me with an expreffion which communicated fomething like delighted *vanity* to my heart.

" Tell her fhe is an angel," faid my father laughing.

" I will

" I will tell her *truth*," replied St. Elmer—

" In the language of flattery," pursued my father.

" Never from *my* lips," returned St. Elmer.

" Be then her mentor, not her seducer," said my father; " vanity is the betrayer of *woman* and the *friend* of man; *we* could do nothing without that agreeable aid-de-camp, St. Elmer, to administer our vows for gospel."

St. Elmer only smiled; he took my hand, which he affectionately pressed, and led me to the carriage.

He

He was nineteen when I last beheld him—now he was three-and-twenty. Fifteen is a dangerous period for a young woman to conceive an attachment for a youth of three-and-twenty; in vain do the prejudices of *age* exclaim, the prejudices of *youth* are incontrovertible; in vain all their reasoning; youth *cannot* see with the eyes of age, and experience only can teach what precept fails to inculcate. "Every age, every station," I believe Rousseau observes in La Nouvelle Heloise, "has its maxims and its virtues; what in some might be prudence, would in others be hypocrisy, and instead of rendering us wise or virtuous, they make us imprudent and guilty, by confounding these characteristic attributes."

I was

I was scarcely welcomed by the Rosendorf with common politeness; indeed her neglect was obvious; and I
quitted the apartment for one more calculated to restore my spirits; I mean the
music-room.

I executed several lively airs with
much taste but no judgment; conscious
of my want of excellence, I was rather
hurt than pleased at beholding St. Elmer
in a listening attitude at the furthermost
door. He approached me, and I immediately ceased.

"I do not ask you to continue,"
said he, "for I wish rather to gratify
my heart than amuse my senses, and I

E 4   prefer

prefer your converfation to your mufic."

I felt my heart involuntarily palpitate, for I felt like a culprit arraigned at the bar of juftice, and fearful his guilty eloquence fhall not avail; I feared St. Elmer's keen inveftigation of my fenti-ments, and dreaded his difcovering the anarchical ftate of my ideas.

It was evidently his intention to fearch my mind, to difcover my ideas on par-ticular fubjects, and fee if they fhrunk from fcrutiny; to trace, as he fince ac-knowledged, the various mazes of my heart, and by leading me through an imperceptible chain of arguments, to analyze my ruling paffion.

" Alas!

" Alas! my dear Cazire," he obferves in fome one of his letters, " dare I acknowledge I did not *then* difcover in you all I wifhed; I found you bewildered in the delufive labyrinths of falfe fentiment, afpiring to be an heroine in fame inftead of virtue, and with a heart capable of the divineft attributes, loft and perverted by this melancholy furor. You poffeffed a fenfitivenefs, which, while it filled me with inexpreffible rapture, bade me tremble for the *wounds* it muft receive; a ftrong imagination and characteriftic enthufiafm gratified my fenfibility, but alarmed m love; for I faw, dear and unfortunate girl, the dangers and fatal errors into which they would precipitate you. Buried beneath

E 5   thofe

those thick pervading clouds, I discovered all that was noble in danger of being destroyed; I saw philanthropy the most refined in want of a guide, ever ready to become the *prey* of the impostor or the *dupe* of the unworthy; a total disregard of *prejudice,* and under that specious mask of *prudence* also, (for there are even *neceʃʃary prejudices,*) a disdain of *all* opinion, and this but too often precedes a desperate contempt of *our own*; a romantic generosity of sentiment, willing to view the most imprudent deeds of others through the false medium of enthusiasm; you had also some very dangerous notions of love; and this passion, when conceived for an *improper* object, is the certain innovator of all principle.

You

You would have fold yourfelf to deftruction for the man who could have gained
your heart; but this, though your fufceptibility was extreme, was fortunately
counteracted by a tenacity of fentiment
and jealoufy of difpofition, that, while it
fhewed at once the delicacy and ardour
of your imagination, would, I fometimes hoped, preferve you from incau-
tioufly bartering your peace for an un-
certain reciprocity of affection.

" I admired you once as an agreeable
child; then, by an eafy natural tranfition,
I *loved* you as an enchanting girl; *then*
I trembled for you, and confidered you
as a beautifully ftupendous pyramid,
which, while it forcibly interefts our

E 6   *admiration,*

admiration, still tinctures it with involuntary horror left its towering grandeur should, from its very *exaltation*, be more liable to fall.''

CHAP. IX.

HABITS BECOME PRINCIPLES.

PLEASED to have engaged the attention of St. Elmer from the reſt of the
company, ſomething whiſpered more
than the ſportiveneſs of infancy muſt
now be his attraction. I felt delighted
and thrown entirely off my guard by the
eaſy careleſſneſs of his manner ; I was
led to ſay more than I had firſt intended,
and then imagining I had gone too far to
retract,

retract answered his pofitions with freedom and unreferve, argued with him on
topics the moft interefting, and at once
betrayed my fallacious fentiments to his
wounded ear.

St. Elmer grew referved; he had difcovered more than he wifhed.—an ample
foil where the dangerous poppy fprung
unmolefted near the gentle rofe, and
threatened to overpower its fweetnefs
with a fubtle *poifon*; he fuffered me to
proceed as I pleafed; I imagined he was
paufing on what I advanced, and felt
chagrined, when taking my hand he faid
with an impreffive fmile,

" And where, my dear Cazire, did
you *learn* all this? what are the books
you perufe?"

I men_

I mentioned hefitatingly fome of my favourite authers, remarkable for the fweet deftruction they conveyed in the garb of fentiment.

He was filent.

I expatiated upon their fancied me-rits.

" I could have *wifhed*," faid St. El-mer at length, " that your tafte for reading had been *better* cultivated; you would *then* have been a creature amiable and fafcinating as you are *now* danger-ous and unfortunate."

Did I hear aright? I turned my eyes full upon St. Elmer, and blufhed the deepeft deepeſt ſcarlet; then I caſt them on the ground—then again upon St. Elmer—then they once more ſought the ground, and, unable to conquer my ſtruggling emotions, unable to recover from the blow which vanity had received, I burſt into tears.

" Cazire?" exclaimed St. Elmer, viſibly affected, and his face crimſoned with emotion, " I conjure you forbear. I cannot endure to ſee a female weep—to ſee *you* weep." He faltered. " For heaven's ſake ceaſe, or with all my boaſted philoſophy you will ſee me diſſolved in ſimilar weakneſs at your feet."

My tears continued—I could not ſtay them.

" Alas!

" Alas! what have I done!" he pursued in an agitated voice, " I have been
too *harsh*, too sudden. Will you not forgive me?" he added, bending over me
with increased emotion, " will you not
pardon me? I have wounded the senfi-
bility I adore—I have given pain to the
moft fufceptible of bofoms. Cazire, I
befeech you extend the olive branch."

I fmiled through my tears upon the
agitation of St. Elmer—I gave him my
hand—his trembled as he received it;
and, incapable of purfuing a converfation which had already coft us both fo
much, he led me as I recovered to the
drawing room * * * * * * *
* * * * * * * * * * * *

It

It was now settled that one year more should terminate my residence at the convent of St. Omer, and I should then take up my abode with my mother.

I left home early the following morning, and St. Elmer accompanied me on horseback to the gates of the monastery.

I know not how logicians will explain it, but though the remembrance of St. Elmer vanished not from me with his presence, though he still dwelt on my mind with something warmer than *friendship*, yet was it something colder than *love*—I did not experience for *him* that passionate sensation which is the invariable attendant of love; I considered him as too *superior* a being to inspire
more

more than a fort of *awful respect*; and I
found myfelf in no danger of imbibing
for him an enthufiaftic and lafting attachment fuch as I have depicted.

During this prefcribed year I received
feveral vifits from my father, always accompanied by St. Elmer. Sometimes
my father would ride a few miles further, and St. Elmer then remained with
me till his return; but never more would
he expofe himfelf to my tears by touching on the flighteft chord that could have
excited them; he heard all I boldly advanced, but heard me with a fmile of
anguifh which more than the moft elo-
quent language fpoke his feelings; fometimes too he brought me books, but he
was fcrupuloufly felect in his offering,
                                    and

and in *that* alone delicately betrayed his
anxiety for the alteration of my sentiments. These shewed the dangers of
fallacious systems, of unrestrained passion and enthusiasm; their doctrines
were the doctrines of reason and of virtue; they pointed out with the finger of
truth the errors in which I had become
involved; and sometimes the melodious
voice of St. Elmer read me aloud a
passage here and there with an emphasis
at once pointed and impressive. I listen-
ed in silence; almost fancied myself *convinced*; when suddenly he ceased, and I
discovered, or imagined I discovered
the whole merit of what I had heard to
consist in the figure, the delivery of the
charming reader. We cannot divest
ourselves of early associations or youthful

ful habits; it was in vain I attempted to
dwell *sincerely* on the books given me by
St. Elmer; I did not find them congenial to my feelings as thofe to which I
had long been habituated, and with renovated eagernefs I refumed my dif-
graced favourites.

CHAP. X.

MELANCHOLY ANTICIPATIONS.

AT length the year terminated; an apartment was prepared for my reception in my mother's house, and the time fixed for my departure from St. Omer's drew rapidly near. I had hoped and expected a visit from St. Elmer previous, but I received only a letter, which ran thus:

" To

" To Cazire.

" I know not in what light you may regard what I am going to say, whether you will deem me officiously *intrusive* or impertinently *severe*; but this I know, that the motives which instigate me I need not blush to *acknowledge*, they are founded in an anxious solicitude (more anxious than it is possible for you to conceive) for your welfare. You have acquired, I perceive, and it is with sorrow I make the observation, a set of ideas, a chain of sentiments, which, if not timely checked, will involve you in *inevitable destruction*. Nay, start not, I will be free; have I not known you from an infant? this, independent of *other* considerations,

fiderations, deeply interefts me in your
happinefs, and fills my bofom with anguifh for your future fate. Already,
young as you are, you broach your
documents with the *pride* of a philofopher without his *prudence*; you have
adopted a certain mode of thinking rather on account of its *eccentricity* than
its *juftice*, and the language of your fentiments is more eloquential than per-
fect.

" But are you aware, my dear Cazire, that while you thus purfue a *meteor*
the broad beam of *reafon* is obfcured?
your imagination takes the lead, and deftroys with its force the weak bloffoms
of rifing intellect. Why fhould powers
like yours become unhappily perverted?
why

why do you prefer rather fwimming in
the glittering whirlpool of deftruction to
laving in the placid waters of rationality.
You travel in fairy-land; all is fiction,
all is madnefs, romance, and folly ; you
tread with the light ftep of an aerial
nymph over rofy parterres, little dreaming of the fnakes which lurk in ambufh
—little dreaming of the watchful ruin
that even *now* gapes for its *heedlefs* prey.
Sometimes above the horizon of wild
enthufiafm appears the fun of reafon ;
gloomy and overcaft it feems, but you
heed it not, and chufe rather to *purfue*
the path of certain danger than *re-trace*
the backward way.

" I forefee from the extreme, the uncontrolled acutenefs of your feelings,

you will have much unhappinefs to encounter; you are a felf-tormentor, and
with ftern and gloomy eye view ever the
darker fide of the picture—your antici-
pations are thofe of a melancholy enthufiaft.

"From the fufceptibility of your
heart you will be involved in dangers of
all dangers the moft imminent—I mean
thofe of *love*—perhaps I fhould fay
paffion.

"From the philanthropy and warmth
of your difpofition, ever ready to attach the *beft* motives to the *worft* actions,
I fear you will meet oftener with *decep-
tion* than *gratitude*. Perhaps you may
hate me for all this, and confider the
dangers,

dangers, which by amplifying on I would warn you of, as the mifanthropical ebullitions of a cynic; but judge lefs harfhly of me; St. Elmer *is* your friend; he would warn you of the delufions of paffion and falfe fentiment, which, like fafcinating treacherous guides, lure along their victim by a meteor flame to the very brink of the precipice.

" I fhall not fee you perhaps for long; your mother, to whom you are now going, fuffers, I am informed by your father, no male vifitants at her refidence, and few of your own fex, therefore all communication, fave by letter, is cut off between us; you will, however, fometimes hear from me if you do not fee me; but no more, I hope,

in

in a ſtrain like this, Cazire; it was a
painful duty, which I felt *impelled* to execute. Adieu!

" I ſhould have ſeen you once ere
your departure, but I dared not attempt
to combat your dangerous eloquence,
aſſiſted by the expreſſion of eyes which
almoſt tempt one to forget their *deluſion*.
Once more adieu !

" Louis St. Elmer."

I will confeſs that the former part of
St. Elmer's letter, from the frightful picture he drew as the effect of my ſentiments,

ments, filled me at firſt with gloomy ſenſations; my fate, as though by a ſudden flaſh, ſeemed unwillingly to *reveal* her future horrid ſtores, and I ſhrunk involuntarily appalled; the latter part, however, proved an antidote; and ſince St. Elmer was fearful of *truſting* himſelf with me, he muſt have felt the truth of my arguments, and dreaded conviction; then was I ſtill right; thus from the very boſom of caution did vanity extract additional honey for its food, and I became more than ever intoxicated with the glittering fabric I had reared; every thing around me appeared to increaſe my deluſion, like the fury of a maniac is augmented by whatever offers to oppoſe it. I viewed St. Elmer as a friend,

F 3　　　notwith-

notwithſtanding I remembered him as the
dear companion of my childhood, but
regarded him with an admiration totally
devoid of love.

CHAP. XI.

YOUTHFUL ENTHUSIASM.

I REACHED the village of Staub as evening fpread around her many-coloured mantle; the fcenery was delightful, and I traced with fportive fancy imaginary joys for my future days. Ah! fad delufive dreams! why did you dance before my laughing hopes? too fatally were all your fairy vifions overthrown, and experience pointed pale and ftern to

the

the bleak defolated heath where they had gamboled.

It was the latter end of June; the air was calm and temperately warm; a red ftreak in the weftern fky reflected its glowing luftre on my countenance—I felt my heart bound in my bofom, and exhilarated by indefinable fenfations. There was a fomething in the atmofphere that would have cheered me, methinks, under ills the moft depreffing. A deep ftillnefs reigned around, and the diftant monaftery receded from my view. As I proceeded, my bufy fancy feemed connecting a chain of improbable events, and I panted involuntarily for a fome-what I could not defcribe; I endeavoured to analyze my wifhes, but in vain;

vain; an ardent defire of attainment, a
meteor that mocked my grafp, an unknown requifite [feemed ftill neceffary,
but neither reafon nor imagination could
identify it.

I fmiled at my own enthufiafm, and
to banifh its influence, looked out for
the cottage of my mother. I beheld at
a diftance its white front emerging from
among the trees, and formed to myfelf a
bower of felicity of which I fhould become the idol.

As I indulged in thefe fairy fancies
the chaife ftopped. I fprang up the
garden, and haftily entering the cottage
beheld, not as I had figured, fmiles of
joy and rapturous welcome, but my

mother,

mother, with gloom and difcontent
written in her afpeƈt, ftanding near a
window, my fifter weeping bitterly in a
corner, and my brother, with a pair of
little hands that might have vied in co-
lour with Othello's, feated on the ground
by her fide, and wiping with a handker-
chief the tears from her cheek.

My entrance caufed a temporary fuf-
penfion of hoftilities. I was fincerely
welcomed by my mother, while my fifter
fufpending her tears, and my brother his
innocent good offices, approached to
furvey me.

I had been the darling of my father,
an inmate in his houfe near his perfon;
was not this fufficient to make me welcome

come to my mother? Never was she
weary of inquiring concerning Arieni—
Did he appear really fond of the Rosendorf? did he prefer her children? did he
ever mention her to me?

I replied to my mother's interroga-
tions as I thought she wished, not as I
believed sincere. I considered with attention the objects round me, I endeavoured to discover the mode of living
which appeared predominant; the result
of my observations were dissatisfaction
and regret. I missed the easy elegance
of my father's house—the peaceful refinement of St. Omer's; and in lieu of
these, a gloomy misanthropy and melancholy *ennui* appeared to reign throughout; there was nothing that renders

seclusion

feclufion from the world delightful; not
a philanthropic pity for, but a hatred of,
mankind, had feemed the refult of this
ifolation. With a fenfation of uneafi-
nefs different to any I had yet experienced, I retired early to my allotted
chamber.

The exhilarating fun beams darted
warm in at the window, the gay birds
carrolled to the morn, and the beauty of
the furrounding landfcape infpired me
with cheerfulnefs; I rofe, and began to
hope the fenfations of the preceding
evening had arifen from fatigue, difcontent, or aught but reality. Determined
to view all with the eye of a philofopher, and accord where I could not remedy, I defcended to the parlour. I
found

found the family affembled; again I was treated with diftinction, again admired; but fpite of all, again I felt the damp ftealing over my heart; for I faid mentally, "When the novelty of my appearance fhall be over, it will be fucceeded by the gloom and unfociability I have only temporarily banifhed."

But a fhort period had elapfed, and my fad predictions were verified. I had no one with whom I could converfe; the means by which I had obtained books were completely cut off; and, add to this, Arieni; who when my mother firft arrived had frequently vifited her, by degrees grew weary of the fad reproaches of an unfortunate deluded wife, and feldom fubjected himfelf to a

view

view of the mournful horrors he had caufed.

Gradually I felt myfelf finking into defpondency; my feelings preyed upon me, and I feared the morning of my days would be fpent in cheerlefs gloom.

In this temperament of mind, reflecting with bitternefs on the cruelty of the Rofendorf who was the occafion of my fadnefs, I walked one morning into the garden behind the houfe; a ftranger, who lived on the adjacent fide, but whom I had never before feen, was carefully watering a few plants; he perceived and faluted me. As he raifed his countenance, not its beauty, but the fingular expreffion

expreffion it contained rivetted my attention. I leaned over the palings, and
feemed obferving his employment, when
it was in reality, if chance permitted, to
fteal another look at his features.

" I love to attend to thefe children
of Nature," faid he, perceiving that I
noticed him ; " ere long the fun reaches
its meridian, and parches them to nothing."

" I thought it cherifhed them," faid I.

" It might do fo," he replied, " were
they better protected ; but now, like a
faithlefs lover, expofed and unfheltered
as they are, his ardency deftroys them.
Here," he continued, plucking a rofe
from

from its fragrant bed, " place this in your bofom, and truft me it will live longer there than its unfortunate neighbour will do here."

" Think you then," faid I, " the fpot you have felected is fo cold ?"

" Its fanctity will preferve it there," he replied. " But can that bofom be already fufceptible of warmth?" continued he, raifing his expreffive eyes to my countenance.

There was nothing in the ftranger's glance—why then did I blufh ?

" Whence is it," purfued he, " that your fex earlier than ours can define its fenfations.

fenfations. The fentiments of a boy at fifteen are unknown to himfelf—a temporary paffion inflames his fenfes—gratification ends it, and fatiety fucceeds; at fifteen your fex can love, can combat their defires, can ftruggle with their feelings, and ultimately conquer; their refinement and their delicacy aim at fomething nobler than fenfual happinefs—they feek to attach the heart, and droop at finding they only intereft the fenfes."

" But may not the heart be feduced through the medium of the fenfes?" faid I.

" Rarely with us," he replied; " poffeffion ends our joys, it is the tomb of love."

" I think,"

" I think," faid I, " the reafon is
this : cuftom authorifes man to feek, to
obtain the gratification of his wifhes—
no ftigma attends his conduct, no cen-
fure deters, the road lies open before
him, ftrewed with flowers and inviting
his fteps ; gratified almoft before he can
analyze his wifhes, there is no room for
him to refine upon them ; and, led by
paffion, he often remains the victim of
its folly. Women, on the contrary,
fhackled by the laws of cuftom, withheld
by worldly prudence, and taught perpe-
tual rebellion againft the whifperings of
Nature, early learn to confine their
wifhes to the filent folitarinefs of their
own bofoms ; they know the fmalleft
lapfe of decorum is attended with ever-
lafting opprobrium, and fhrinking they

retire

retire from the hydra-headed monster
raised by custom; by dwelling on their
deep concealed emotions they learn at
length to refine upon them, to shake off
as it were the sensualism of Nature, become nobly disinterested in their love,
and gradually change it into a refined
friendship. It is true ere they can ac-
complish this they must learn Concealment, the mother of Art; they must
exchange for it her lovely sister Nature.
But custom commands—the world will
have it so—perhaps we become better
and happier than you are by the law."

The stranger did not immediately reply; he examined me attentively, and
appeared surprised. I smiled—it seemed

to

to awaken him from his reverie, and bending over the palings he faid,

" I entreat you to continue ; you are the only female for fix years I have found it poffible to converfe with."

" Indeed," faid I, " I pity you fincerely, and thank you in the name of the fex at large."

" What age are you ?" inquired he fmiling.

" Sixteen."

" Do you love reading?"

He

He did indeed ' touch upon the ftring' on which hung all my wifhes.

" It is the only thing I do love," I eagerly rejoined.

" I am forry to hear you fay fo," he replied ; " if you had a lover you would be happier, he would be"——

" Miferable," interrupted I, " miferable would be the man I loved."

The ftranger fmiled incredulously.

" My tenacious fpirit," purfued I, " my high ideas of what we love ought to be, my defpair if for a moment I thought he did not prefer me to every

other

other woman, to himfelf, to the world,
would tend to make him miferable, me
diftracted. It would not be cold pro-
feffions which could content me—it
would not be abfurd encomiums on my
mind or perfon—it would not be luke-
warm affection, unmeaning compliments;
no; his heart, his mind, his feelings, his
fentiments, muft all be congenial to mine,
his eyes, his actions muft declare his
love, his idolatry; he muft adore me
with enthufiafm, fhun, deteft thofe whom
I hated, admire, efteem thofe I loved,
think no facrifice too great for me, not
his life if mine could be preferved, and
defpife even that if I exifted no longer;
know no happinefs but in my fociety,
lament to quit and joy in returning to it,
watch over my couch in ficknefs, and
droop

droop when I grieved, liften with tranfport to my flighteft wifhes, let nor *ennui*
nor fatiety blaft our peace, but look on
me as his world, his treafure, and his
life. Never, never could I meet a being who would love me thus; none other
could poffefs my love; better then never tafte the dangerous ftream but in
its higheft, pureft ftate, or inevitable
wretchednefs would be our mutual lot;
for I difdain the thought of a 'luke-warm
attachment,' a ' fincere regard!' "

" And would you love as you require
to be loved?" faid the ftranger ear-
neftly.

" Or I fhould not dare require it," I
rejoined.

rejoined. " I would voluntarily con-
fign myfelf to deftruction to purchafe
happinefs for the being who could love
me thus."

" Young and innocent enthufiaft,"
exclaimed the ftranger, " pity the vile
world fhould chill the ardor of fuch
fentiments; but alas! you cannot mix
with its miferable inhabitants without
imbibing their mercenary doctrines;
like wretches infected with the plague,
no purity can refide among them, inevitable contamination is the refult of
affociating with them."

" They never can change my fentiments," faid I.

" Sad

" Sad experience will convince you
you have reared for yourself a fairy fabric; bitter will be to you its gradual
yet fure deftruction."

" You are a mifanthropift," faid I.

" I am a veteran in the fchool of adverfity," he replied; " and though I
have fuffered deeply by my companions,
I yet view them with no angry eye; pity
for their misfortunes is my firft fenfation,
contempt for the errors which generate
them is my fecond."

" You are a philofopher then,"
faid I.

The

The ſtranger ſmiled, and remembering how long I had been converſing
with him, " Adieu!" I cried, " I ſtand
no chance with a philoſopher."

CHAP. XII.

THE PHILOSOPHER DEFEATED.

AFTER this I went more frequently into the garden. Fribourg (fo was the ftranger called) was always in his. My converfations with him became frequent, and I fought his fociety with avidity as my only refource from *ennui*. ·His perfon was above the middling height, and poffeffing an air of dignity which feemed to befpeak the independent majefty of

his

his intellect; his countenance was of
that expreffive caft giving the idea of
fuperiority; dark and piercing eyes,
which feemed at once to fearch and underftand the foul, illumined with their
glowing luftre the flight vermillion of his
cheek; when he fmiled it was with an
expreffion penfive and fevere, as though
deeply he had felt the hand of forrow,
but fcorned the impotency of complaint;
his forehead feemed the feat of grandeur
in its towering form; his intire afpect
was fafcination itfelf, his age about
eight-and-twenty.

His ideas on every fubject were un-
circumfcribed by common opinions; he
attacked unhefitatingly the received doctrines of ages, defpifed cuftom, and
formed

formed his actions from the refult of his own inferences: his pleafure feemed in differing from others; eftablifhed laws he confidered prejudices; the principles he avowed were dangerous and feductive, he affirmed they were the offspring of cool difcrimination and difpaffionate reflection, the dictates of nature, reafon, and common fenfe; and yet Fribourg had acted contrary to his theory, he had voluntarily bound himfelf by the moft arbitrary law. Fribourg was married—had been married for fix years. One evening when he was inveighing againft the tyranny and abfurdity of cuftom, I afked him, with a fmile half ferious half farcaftic, what had ever induced him to yield to it?

" Necef-

" Neceffity !" he replied.

" Could Fribourg meanly facrifice his feelings and his fentiments to intereft !"

" Man is the creature of predicament," he anfwered. " I loved Elinor, and found no path open to my happinefs but yielding a portion of my independence. I thought the gain worthy of the facrifice; but it could never influence my ideas; it was a ftep productive of no revolution in my fentiments, nor accorded to but as it forwarded a wifh."

" Think you fo lightly then of a facred ceremony ?"

" It

" It is a ceremony," anfwered he,
" invented by men; Nature knows it
not, therefore it is contemptible; in-
conftancy and licentioufnefs firft rendered it neceffary, the perverted ftate of
fociety ftamped it with the feal of law;
it exifts now as well for thofe who defpife as thofe who need it; invented for
the vulgar many, it fhackles all alike, and
ftamps with unjuft opprobrium thofe who
difdain acceding to it."

" But would you fubvert the prefent
order of fociety, could you fubftitute a
better ?"

" Undoubtedly. I would not fix a
boundary to love; I would not fay, ' fo
far muft you extend, and no further.'

The

The sexes should be linked by affection, not law. When that ceafes, how shall we fill the dreary vacuum? by mutual difguft, or affected regard? For two perfons to be linked together when hearts have long fince feparated, is raifing a wall of impregnable ftrength to fecure a decayed building.

" But at this rate you would new-model the univerfe."

" I would, if it were poffible, and think it would be benefited by the change."

" How could you ever introduce," faid I, " (allowing for a moment the juftice

uſtice of your opinion,) ſo vaſt, ſo mul-
iplied a reform?"

" The growth of perfection," he re-
urned, " muſt be gradual ; the arts and
ciences were ſo."

" I do not think your project feaſible;
ou would turn the world into a ſavage
vilderneſs. In obviating laws which are
nly tremendous to the profligate and
1e baſe, you would entirely baniſh
ivilization, and the virtuous few would
ventually become the victims of bar-
arous innovations and deſtructive irre-
ularity. You remind me of thoſe ſan-
uinary rebels who ſought to hurl a
eaceful monarch from his throne to

G 5   eſtabliſh

establish a monster of their own creation, whose vices and whose indolence
render them obnoxious to society, and
who willingly profited by the general
devastation to attain a guilty eminence
on the mangled bodies of their fellow-
creatures; blood alone could satisfy
their thirsty souls; heated by dwelling
on the fancied injustice they experienced,
they longed to wade through the purple
current, to gorge their hearts with mur-
der, and sink to their own gloomy level
those whom they could not rise to
equal."

" Even if a slight reform were possible to be effected, better far neglect i
than wade through seas of blood to its
completion

completion. Truft me, in attempting to mend you would only deftroy—it is undermining mountains to level a molehill."

" You talk the language," anfwered Fribourg, " of one in love with fecurity and fearful the flighteft change fhould endanger it. But to return; marriage, for inftance; you who defire fuch unbounded enthufiafm in love, do you, I afk, ever obferve the flighteft fymptoms of it in a married life? With all your boafted love of order, wretchedly indeed would you fuftain the character of a wife. What I would propofe is, to allow no room for fatiety to enter. When two of oppofite fexes can no longer be

every

every thing to each other—when the
prefence of a third becomes neceffary as
a charm to exclude the fpeĉtre *ennui—*
when no longer they meet with rapture
and divide with grief—then would I
have them feparate, and not till then."

" Better then," cried I, "for them
never to unite, than already, ere they
have even tafted the happinefs of affociating, provide againft a neceffity for its
continuance; it is ạdmitting a doubt of
affeĉtion, it is outraging the very nature
of love to ftipulate fo early for its freedom; it is unequivocally faying, ' let us
not bind ourfelves beyond the poffibility
of retraĉting. Cold-hearted, wretched
fecurity! No, no, Fribourg; poor indeed

deed muſt be the love that would not ſeek out a tie more ſtrong even than marriage, (if ſuch exiſted,) and delight to be riveted in that. The inſtances of unhappineſs you adduce would exiſt in any ſtate; they could not love before marriage who would not always love; they then ſhould never have been united—they were not deſtined for each other."

"And what muſt be the love, my young enthuſiaſt, which needs a tie ſo ſtrong? Come, come, you are led away by your feelings; hereafter we will purſue the ſubject, and I do not deſpair of your converſion."

"Perverſion you ſhould ſay, Fribourg;

bourg; the truth is, you cannot purſue
the argument, therefore I willingly admit a truce, and give you leave to rally
your forces againſt next we meet."

CHAP. XIII.

THE CONFESSION.

WHILE I was difcourfing with Fribourg, and combating his arguments, I felt as though I had reafon on my fide ; yet I will confefs the novelty of his tenets made me frequently dwell on them; by fo doing they gradually impreffed my mind, and I fometimes believed, as he had faid, in my converfion. The natural inconfiftency of my charafter was

fuch,

fuch, that I feldom viewed an opinion
twice in the fame light; what I one day
believed an immutable truth admitted
the next of variation, and conviction was
the refult of reflection only till it was
difplaced by a later idea. So many
circumftances methought occurred to
make me doubt of any general defini-
tion, that I almoft imagined there were
no fixed principles, nor any pofition not
liable to be found imperfect in different
predicaments; vice or virtue might even
be defective terms in certain fituations;
and thus, from the mutability of my own
ideas, was a channel open for the innovations of others.

I refolved not to fhrink from the arguments of Fribourg; to him it might
imply

imply a doubt of the juſtice of my own, of the ſtrength ot my principles, which I did not deſire him to aſcertain. Deter-mined to hear all, I daily laid myſelf more open to the boldneſs of his reaſon-ings, for I judged if right I muſt ever find arguments to oppoſe him, and retire with added ſtrength from oppoſition; if wrong, why ſhould I dread conviction? I reflected thus; and perhaps I ſought excuſes to continue my interviews with Fribourg; perhaps I felt a pleaſure in his ſociety; I dia not dare acknowledge to myſelf, for Fribourg was married; and unleſs I adopted the freedom of his tenets, to indulge too far even that pleaſure would be criminal. I would not inveſtigate my ſentiments further, eſt rigid prudence ſhould have bade me forſwear forfwear his fociety, at that time my chief, my only confolation.

Not unfrequently was Fribourg accompanied by a young nobleman called Count Lindorf. I was fomewhat piqued at this, for I thought had he wifhed fingly for my fociety he would have deemed every other an intrufion. But to revenge myfelf for this, I fometimes came accompanied by a female; but was this manœuvre really dictated by a fpirit of revenge, or the mere fineffe of growing predilection to engage from us the attention of Count Lindorf?

Sometimes, however, he tortured me with his notice; baffling my every endeavour to decline it, Fribourg appeared

to

to remark and feel gratified at my ftra-
tagem. He took occafion to fay to me
when for a moment the Count had left
us,

" I am forry that ever I introduced
Lindorf to you; he follows me like my
fhadow, he watches my entrance into
the garden, and never fails to accompany me."

" He feems a charming young man,"
faid I.

" He is a very dangerous fellow. I
would advife you to beware of him."

" Why did you bring him with
you?"

He

" He refides with me, and I cannot avoid it—he forces himfelf on me."—

Juft then the Count returned, and ended our dialogue. On my return into the houfe I found a letter for me from an unknown correfpondent. It ran thus:

" I entreat you to be lefs frequent in your vifits to the garden. I fee a gloomy train of evils likely to enfue. You are young and enthufiaftic, Fribourg fpecious and infinuating; already Cazire loves him. With faddened eye I look forward to a melancholy termination of your prefent conduct. Fribourg is married—what then can you hope? Think but for a moment, deluded girl; would

you

you facrifice to the tranfitory pleafure of infpiring him with a reciprocal paffion the happinefs of an unfortunate, doting wife? would you call down the curfes of his children? Think but of your own mother—her misfortunes and yours are entailed by the defertion of an hufband. Yet forbear while you have power—fee him no more; and fince you cannot conquer temptation, learn to fly it.

" ARIEL."

Who was it that, thus affuming the empire of my conduct, dared to arraign my actions? Was it St. Elmer?—impoffible. He ftill occafionally correfponded with me, but it was unlike his hand-

hand-writing, and more unlike his ſtyle.
The letters I had of late received from
him were in general ſhort, lively, and
for the moſt part accompanied with elegant ſelections from modern authors,
pieces of muſic, or original drawings.
Never more had he ventured a letter in
the ſtyle of the laſt which I tranſcribed.
So far from dictating to me a line of
conduct, he ſeemed totally ignorant of
my every purſuit. He reſided at a conſiderable diſtance. Yet who could this
cenſor be? one evidently who knows
me—one dwelling with me almoſt in the
houſe it ſhould appear. It was in vain
I attempted to aſcertain the author—I
could fix with probability on no one—I
knew no one—I converſed with no one
but my family, Fribourg, and Lindorf.

As

As I continned turning it in my hand I
faw a few lines which, from being on
the inner page, had efcaped my notice:

" Your letters will be in future
placed at the bottom of the garden—
chance will direct you to them."

Notwithftanding, however, the purport of this letter, it failed of its intended effect; it did indeed open my
eyes on the danger I was incurring;
but I was like one enjoying a peaceful
flumber rudely awakened by an alarm of
fire, who fees around him the fpreading
flames, and finding it impoffible to
efcape, croffes his arms upon his bofom,
and voluntarily refigns himfelf to deftruction.   I knew not that I loved Fribourg.

bourg. Was it then ſo apparent that a
ſtranger could perceive it?—it was too
late then to ſtruggle againſt the tide.
Thus did I convert the very knowledge
of danger into an excuſe for continuing
in it.

Muſing one evening in the garden
upon a late converſation with Fribourg,
wherein he had convinced me that to
avoid that which is denominated ſin it is
only neceſſary to follow the natural im-
pulſes of the heart, I little dreamt of
meeting with him, for it was later than
ever we had before converſed. The
moon had riſen, the evening was chill;
ſuddenly he glided from behind ſome
trees.

" Come

" Come nearer," he cried, as at a distance I regarded him with a smile. " I have traverfed this day an extent of country that would have unfitted me for any thing but fleep, had I not, afcending to my bed-room, difcerned Cazire through the window."

" I beg," faid I, " I may not fruf-trate your intentions."

" I have told you before," he replied, " I am a necefitarian. I could not avoid defcending and now I cannot retire; therefore feat yourfelf as near as poffible to thefe monaftic gratings, I will do the fame, and let us converfe awhile."

" Pardon me," I replied, " it is too

VOL. I.   H   late,

late, and you muſt neceſſarily be fa-
tigued."

" Cazire, I entreat you to acqui-
eſce?"

I ſtill heſitated.

" Perhaps I may not ſoon again requeſt a ſimilar favor."

I heſitated no longer—in a moment I
was ſeated near him; my heart panting
with a thouſand nameleſs ſenſations;
fear and an expectation of I knew not
what were uppermoſt.

" You muſt enter this garden no
more,"

more," said Fribourg at length, gazing on me with tender earnestness.

" No! Do you find the evenings too cold then?" asked I.

" Alas! no!" he answered with a peculiar emphasis.

I blushed, and remained silent. He continued,

" Do not detest me, Cazire—do not look upon me as the vilest of men.— Contrary to my own ideas I have endeavoured long to struggle against a passion which daily, which hourly becomes stronger—either you must love, Cazire, or for ever banish me your presence."

While

While Fribourg was fpeaking, my ideas had fucceeded each other with fo much rapidity, my heart beat fo violently, and my whole foul had received fuch an agitating fhock—a tranfport fo unknown, fo fudden, that I ftill remained incapable of anfwering. To be loved by Fribourg! it was a fomething fo defired, fo unhoped, fo delightful, fo feduftive, I could not fpeak.

" Cazire," he faid, his voice finking in a tender cadence, " Cazire, can you look upon me."

He drew my hand over the railings which feparated us, and preffing it fervently to his heart, looked at me with a befeeching beſeeching languor that ſpoke in novel accents to my ſoul.

I felt his heart beat hard beneath my hand—I felt him remove it, and tremblingly his glowing lips were riveted upon it. The action rouſed me, and in hurried accents I exclaimed,

" Let me go, Fribourg, for Heaven's ſake. You know I muſt not—dare not —Cruel"—

I ſtruggled to unlooſe my hand.

" I obey " he ſaid, letting it go. " I truſt to your mercy, Cazire, to your generoſity. Fly me not, but grant me ſome reply."

H 3   " What

" What can I say, Fribourg. You know the avowal is—is—"

" Is what?" interrupted Fribourg with emotion.

" Criminal for you to make and me to hear."

" Prejudice, miserable innovator of the finest movements of the heart, why should thy chill influence ever intervene to blast the promised joy! Oh! Cazire, how can you give utterance to the term criminal? Alas! no! cold-hearted, prudential girl, you are guided by systematic frigidity, to the world you yield your feelings and your wishes—to the
world

world you leave the arbitration of your
actions."

" Forbear, Fribourg, cruel and unjuſt
to load me thus. I yield but to my
ideas of duty, not the world."

" Miſtaken girl, it is to the barbarous
policy of cuſtom you are ſubjeƐt. Born
with every ſentiment to ennoble and delight, gifted with ſtrength of mind to
deſpiſe the vulgar errors of mankind,
poſſeſſed of an emanation of ſoul that
ſhould have ſhot triumphant through the
gloomy miſts of ignorance and folly,
yet has the fair germ been blaſted in its
earlieſt green, yet has it been warped
and ſmothered by the prevailing ſyſtems
of an illiberal perverted world."

H 4   " Not

" Not willingly have I refigned myfelf the victim you defcribe.   No, Fribourg, my unbiaffed heart, my moft unbounded enthufiafm, the furtheft limits
of unfettered fentiment, never could lead
me to confider as prejudice the injury I
might caufe another.   How can it be
guiltlefs to ftab with keeneft agony the
bofom of a wife? How can it be guiltlefs to heap deftruction on your children?
Forbear! Have I not a continual picture before my eyes of the cruel confe-
quences of fuch actions? do not I fee a
mother, fcarcely paft the bloom of youth,
a miferable exile from the fociety fhe
might have graced? buried in ungenial
obfcurity the dawning talents of her
children formed for the pride and hope
of an united family? do I not feel myfelf

felf a wretched alien from a father's
heart? do I not load with endlefs curfes
the diabolical woman whofe cruelty hath
caufed this lift of horrors?"

As I fpoke thus the eldeft boy of Fribourg, about four years of age, came
running towards us. The child loved
me, and no fooner perceived me in converfe with his father, than he got over
the fence to embrace me in his little
arms. Convulfively I preffed the innocent to my bofom.

"Sweet boy," faid I with mixed emotions, "could I thus look upon thee,
thus receive thy fpotlefs careffes, if I
were plotting thy ruin? Could I gaze on
thee without blufhing, unconfcious,

H 5   guiltlefs

guiltlefs child? with one hand prefs thee
to my heart, and aim with the other the
fanguinary blow of treachery at thy mother's life?   No, no! it is not the privilege of guilt to meet the innocent fmile—
it is not the privilege of guilt to contem-
plate a victory over felf.'

I burft into a paffion of tears, and
turned afide.

" Return into the houfe," faid Fribourg fternly to the child.

" Are not you coming too, father?"
he artlefsly replied; " my mother is
waiting to play over for you a fong I
have juft taught her."

" Return

" Return into the houfe," repeated
Fribourg.

The poor child was retiring; when
calling him back,

" Play awhile in the garden," I faid,
" till your father is ready."

For perhaps I experienced fear, the
immediate attendant of guilt, left the
boy fhould mention to Elinor it was I
detained her hufband. I dreaded too
left the knowledge of this fhould mortify
the pride or hurt the tender feelings of
a wife.

" You determine then," purfued the

unaltered Fribourg, "you determine on pursuing your fallacious system?"

" Whatever it may cost me, Fribourg —I do."

" Farewell then, Cazire; for from this hour we must part for"——

" Forbear the conclusion!" I exclaimed, blushing at the eagerness I betrayed. " Debar me not of your society," I tremulously added.

" You cannot love me, Cazire. We must"——

" I do—I must.—Oh! cruel Fribourg, to wring from me the guilty acknowledg-

knowledgment. * * * * * Farewell!" I continued, my voice broken
with emotion, " I can bear this fcene
no longer." And rufhing from the garden I fought my chamber.

CHAP. XIV.

THE SOPHIST.

SLEEP was a stranger to my wearied eyes.!—I dared not trust myself to review my conduct: I felt its inconsistency, its impropriety, but in vain; stronger than all I felt my love! my brain whirled in anarchy, and the earliest dawn was my signal for rising. I hurried into the garden; and ere I could recollect how I got there, I was gazing with raptured eye.

eye upon the feat, the railings, the very
fpot where Fribourg had told me that
he loved *me*. I thought over every
word he had uttered; I retraced every
look, every action: fond memory re-
verted to his fpeaking figure, his expreffive countenance, as he had faid, I
love you. Alas! how dangerous are the
firft approaches of paffion to an enthufiaftic fufceptible foul! I was deep in
my vifionary bower, and perceived not
that Fribourg ftood before me.

" So early rifen from your bed!" faid
a melodious voice.

I turned, but did not look at him.

" Was

" Was it an uneafy one ?" he added, fmiling with ill-concealed delight.

" I thought you did not intend feeing me any more?" I replied without noticing his remark; " how comes it you fo foon relent?" returning his fmile.

" I have been confidering," replied he, " that life is fhort; if then in *my* path are ftrewn fome rofes, why fhould I pafs them by to pluck the thorns?"

" Becaufe the thorns," I replied, " will only give probationary wounds; the rofes are ftrewn in our path to try our fortitude, and teach us to avoid temptation; beneath them lurks the poifonous

fonous adder; they are far more dangerous than the thorns."

"And more inviting," he replied,
"life is too fhort to admit of thefe de-
ftinctions. Let us then, Cazire, pluck
the rofes while we *can*; the fenfelefs
bigot only would prefer the thorns—
ere he can reach the rofe—he *dies*."

"A brighter rofe awaits him," returned I; "a glorious immortality!"

"What would you think," faid Fribourg, "of a ftarving wretch, who beholding within his reach a cluster of
ripened grapes looked higher, and determined to remain unfatisfied till thofe
above him had attained maturity?"

"I fhould

" I should think him," replied I, unconscious to what his question tended, " incapable of such forbearance, ridiculous in aiming at it."

" Thus then it is," he answered; " of the present we are assured—of the future we have but a vague and imperfect idea; philosophy nor reason can ascertain the nature of our rewards or punishments; the highest stretch of human intellect cannot soar beyond a given point; there our researches stop; reason finds itself inadequate to identify its own conceptions; it can attach probability to none."

" The future," returned I, alarmed at finding to what his inference tended;

" is

" is purpofely *hid* from our knowledge, to render ftronger and more firm our truft in the Deity; becaufe the weak powers of man cannot pierce beyond the clouds. Is he to arraign the fupe-riority of the Being who refides there? The knowledge you lament as unobtain-able, would be beyond the power of man to bear; he is too inferior a creature to be trufted with perceptions fo divine. He knows not how to exift; he is even ignorant of how the formation of his own ftructure renders him capable of fuch and fuch exertions——the ephe-mera of an hour——the prefumptuous defpot of a day! To releafe him from his ignorance would diveft him of his faith: he beholds the univerfe formed for his ufe; he fees around him the

glorious

glorious presence of a Divinity; he feels
it in his heart, in his senses: he can account for all he sees by believing in
God; why then should he doubt so wonderful a Being, possessed of every great
and noble attribute? why was he en-
dowed with the instinctive idea? how
came it ever into his brain, that he
would fain expel it? By believing that
which we cannot comprehend; by feeling assured of its truth only, can we expect hereafter to have it ascertained."

" The language of education, not
one natural idea! Cazire, more reflection, uncircumscribed by scholastic rules,
would teach you to argue differently:
to believe what we cannot comprehend,
to doubt what reason whispers, implies
a Being

a Being relying on our ignorance for our faith; implies too that a higher portion of intellect, by enlarging our ideas and developing the mysteries which now baffle our conception, would show us the fallacy of our present system of belief, the impotency and folly of any enacted religion. Besides, it is not you and I only who differ; most nations differ from each other in their laws, their systems, and their faith Why, if you would support your argument, was not an universal religion given to mankind? All cannot be right; and if all are wrong save one, are we to infer the partiality of a Supreme Being to a chosen few ? are we to infer that all professing a different persuasion from this one, yet all pursuing the system of worship in which they

they were originally taught, shall be
cursed for their involuntary apostacy to
the true? Yet how, in the midst of such
variety, shall we determine right? and if
every nation may pursue its own code,
it follows that religion is the fabrication
of man, not of divine institution; or
does it imply a different God for every
different mode of worship? Why then
must individuals accord, if nations differ? I have as much ground for the
pursuance of my own system as you for
yours, or the Indian for his."

" Fribourg," said I, " pursue this no
further, lest for ever you sink in my
esteem. On this point my principles
are immutable, perhaps on this alone;
for it is a received maxim with me—no

one

one wishes to doubt the sacred truth of
religion, or the unquestionable being of
a God, but such as seek a licenfe for depravity, and who willingly would disbe-
lieve a future ftate, fearlefsly to outftrip
the boundaries of virtue, and dread no
late account. It appears to me as
though a maniac only could give utterance to fuch ideas. How fhall we account for the formation of the univerfe?
for the regular fucceffion of the feafons?
of day and night, of infcrutable time, of
birth, exiftence, and death? how fhall
we account for the varied chain of wonders that daily ftrike upon our fenfes,
but by attributing all to a Power un-
fathomable as the works which we be-
hold? Chance, fay you and others of
your fect, originally produced them.—
Chance?

Chance?—'tis well—we differ then about the name alone; for you, as well as me, allow a firft caufe. Chance was never yet the parent of continued regularity.; its effects could not pierce through the lengthened mifts of time, and diffeminate for a duration of ages. The name you have given your firft caufe is erroneous, is abfurd; it is Chance you dignify inftead of God.—Oh! how could we even live if we poffeffed not faith, and confequently hope? how bear affliction, pain, and all the numerous ills that follow in fad proceffion on the life of man? Think you that life affords happinefs fufficient to render unneceffary the cheering hope of future greater blifs? Again, you fay nations differ in their mode of worfhip :

in

in the *mode* they do, not in the *purport*—
all worſhip *a God*—they worſhip him
under various denominations—like you,
they differ only in the name, agreeing
all in the main point. God is too juſt,
too noble, to curſe thoſe who variouſly
addreſs him ; as well you might ſay one
language only can be pure. God re-
gards the heart, not the formation of the
prayer—it is the actions of the man, his
ſentiments, his ſoul, and not his mode
of worſhip—the untutored Negro and
the civilized Chriſtian will alike be heard
by an impartial judge ; the grievances,
the unjuſt ſtripes of the former, ſhall not
paſs unrevenged, nor the virtuous actions
of the latter unrewarded. But how came
we upon this ſubject ? it is too ſerious—
let us change it."

VOL. I.   I   " Willingly.

" Willingly. But are you then ſtill averſe, Cazire, to my enjoying the roſes which grow beneath my feet?"

" If you mean literally the roſes, no; if metaphorically, I am."

" Why then were they placed ſo near me? are they ſtrewn in our way but to be paſt? is it in your ſyſtem to become ſtoical to every earthly good? why have we paſſions, wiſhes, or inclinations?"

" To conquer them, Fribourg. If we were never tempted we could never tri-umph; where is the merit of victory if we are not ſolicited to yield?"

" You are determined then to con-quer,

quer, and teach me forbearance likewife.
Since we have inclinations only to make
us miferable, and paffions only to inftruct us how to conquer them; crown
your happinefs with the barren wreath
of victory, over pleafure, liberty, and
love."

" Liberty and love! Alas!" fighed I,
" I cannot give you the firft—you dare
not offer me the fecond."

" And if I durft, you are above
temptation, Cazire. But tell me, if
without injuring in the fmalleft point
fociety or the individual, you could follow a fyftem of independence, would
you ftill hefitate?"

" If

" If it was myself alone I injured by the purfuance of an inclination, I might feel authorifed to follow it."

Fallacious doctrine, as I have fince difcovered, and dangerous latitude to indulge in; fo long as example can influence the manners of fociety, or taint the habits of an individual, fo long will it be unjuft to adopt a felf-created fyftem.— Man can never be independent of his fellows—he dare not commence free agent. In wandering from the beaten track, without any guide but the *ignis fatuus* of fancied right, we fall, and drag along with us many an unconfcious wretch, following with imagined fecurity our footfteps, the fate even of thoufands may be remotely affected. But I did

not

not think thus in the exigency of the moment; and Fribourg continued,

" At leaſt, then, to ſee me, to converſe to walk with me, can injure no one but myſelf; will you refuſe me this?"

" Shall I not debar your wiſe of her juſt right," I heſitatingly rejoined, " your ſociety, Fribourg?"

" Do you make me the property of any one?" replied he haughtily, " do you talk of fettering my ſteps, of confining my perſon?"

" Surely, Fribourg, you would be encircled by your family if not walking or converſing with me?"

" Conſci-

" Conscientious girl, Long ere you
entered the village I was absent for whole
days; the very night bounded not my
wanderings. Lately I have been more
at home, conscious perhaps my happiness
was nearer. But say, do you consent?
The busy world will presently be stirring,
and see us thus early in converse; for
myself I care not; you have not yet
learned to despise its formalities."

" Alas! Fribourg, is concealment ne-
cessary where no wrong is meant?" "

" But what the heart feels innocent
the world condemns, and you cannot
delineate its fine-drawn sensations to the
vulgar eye. To avoid then equally its
censure or its misconstruction, it is better
retire from its scrutiny. Here," he continued,

tinued, " at your leisure you may peruse this," giving me a paper, " it is a poem to the Mountain Violet."

As I stretched forth my hand to receive it, he pressed and gently retained it.

" Do you walk this evening?"

I hesitated.

" Where?"

" Any where with you," he eagerly rejoined. " Come, do not deny me every thing, Cazire."

I 4   " I grant

" I grant too much already, Fribourg—but—I·will come."

" Be in the avenue leading to the
foreſt at night—it is moonlight—you
need not fear.'

" And if it were as Cimmerian ob-
ſcurity, is not Fribourg my protection?"

His eyes ſparkled with pleaſure as I
ſaid this. I was happy to have cheered
him; he imprinted a kiſs upon my hand
—and we ſeparated.

When I returned to my chamber I
peruſed the following poem:

TO

TO THE MOUNTAIN VIOLET.

Sweet fragile flower, that bloom'ft unfought,
  And bloom ft by many an eye unfeen,
Thy worth awakes my penfive thought—
  Fit fubject for the Mufe's theme.

Thy lowly head with patience bent
  Unfhelter'd to the nothern blaft,
As fiercely by the whirlwinds fent,
  Nor deign'd to crufh thee as they paft.

Expanding wild, thy rich perfume
  Impregnates round th' unhallow'd air,
That reeklefs of thy virgin bloom
  Sweeps not o'er thee more mild or fair.

Now brighten'd by the morning ray
  Luxuriant fpreads thy grateful breaft;
Now evening comes with tyrant fway,
  And chills thy little form to reft.

Sweet

Sweet emblem of the soul-fraught mind,
  Expos'd life's keenest storms to bear,
Yet, like thee, tenderly refin'd
  And shrinking from ungenial air.

Like thee too, from the vulgar eye
  The chasten'd mind shall live forlorn;
And though no kindred soul may sigh,
  In solitude there's none to scorn.

The ray which gilds with lucid gleam
  Is the firm mind which none can wrest;
The evening chill, which shrouds the beam,
  The sad reflexions of the breast.

Dear flower, be thou my favorite sweet;
  I'll rear with care thy lowly head;
Save thy soft breast from guardless feet,
  And court young zephyrs to thy bed.

Yet if perchance in evil hour
  Some lawless hand invade thy shrine,
Or nightly blast with ruthless power
  Sap the short life which might be thine;

                                        Ah

Ah! then with sad regret I'll kneel,

 And try thy beauties dimm'd to cheer;

If vain, alas! my hopes I feel,

 I'll dead, embalm thee with a *tear*.

CHAP. XV.

THE SOPHISTRY OF PASSION.

FAITHFUL to my appointment, I found myſelf at eight in the avenue. Fribourg was already there. He linked my arm in his, and drew me on. How ſwift the moments paſs when we would have them linger. Already through the diſtant crevices of the ſurrounding cottages beamed the evening taper; light no longer trembled on the mountain top;

no

no more the blue mists of even obscured
the surrounding sky, but the pale moom-
beams shed their sentimental radiance
on the sleeping beauty of the scene. I
could not have imagined half an hour
had elapsed, but the even pace of time
neither slackening nor increasing with
our wishes, had already told two hours.
The distant tinkling of the village bell
alarmed me.

" Can it be so late, Fribourg?" I exclaimed.

" Has the time then passed unheeded
by you?" he replied.

" It has indeed. Let us make
amends," I continued, " for our negli-
gence;"

gence ;" and hurried onwards. As we
came within sight of the avenue I separated from him, and returned home.

The following morning I promised
again to be in the avenue. For some
months this dangerous intercourse continued, and when for the whole day we
had not seen each other, the avenue at
eight witnessed our delighted meeting.
It was one evening when, as usual, I
had flown to the appointed spot; for
Fribourg had long since silenced my
scruples on that subject, he had said that
on me alone depended the domestic
tranquillity of an innocent wife, that as
I raised or depressed his soul by my compliance or refusal of what he termed his
guiltless wishes, the effects would be
perceptible

perceptible in his family. Happy in being thus furnished with excuses for the
wildness of a disastrous passion, I suf-
fered its fatal innovations with something so like pleasure that all my philosophy became powerless to resist it. On
this evening then, encountering Fribourg, methought he seemed overcast
with an uncommon sorrow; not as usual
his extended arms and eager eyes had
anticipated my approach, scarcely he
increased his pace to welcome me, and
as he drew my arm through his, I heard
him deeply sigh.

" Fribourg!" I exclaimed with beat-
ing heart, and pressing his hand to my
trembling lips, " Fribourg, what has
happened? whence the gloom so visible
upon

upon thofe features. Tell me—tell me quick or I cannot fupport myfelf."

My agitation almoft incapacitated me from ftanding; I encircled his arm with my clafped hands, and my head drooped upon it.

" Cazire, my love," he faid, " my only charm in exiftence, be not alarmed, I am not gloomy—you miftake, indeed you—nothing has happened—you"—

He feated me on a bank befide us, and folded me to his breaft, fcarcely confcious I fuffered him to retain me in his arms. For the firft time our lips met—it thrilled in liquid fire to my heart—I felt the ardent blufhes of my
cheek,

cheek, and returned with tranfport hi-
therto unknown, the kifs of Fribourg.——
Amazed, delighted, he preffed me clofer
to his throbbing bofom——his head fank
on mine——for fome minutes we remained
in the firft ecftatic trance of love * *
* * * * * * * * * *

Suddenly I recollected the wild involuntary tranfport I had indulged in——
the firft moft ferious latitude I had given
my feelings. With blufhes no more of
ardent paffion, but fhame and confcious
guilt, with deep regret and almoft horror for my conduct, I felt how dangerous
it is to admit the flighteft toleration of
error to the heart. I endeavoured to
rife——the fafcinating countenance of
Fribourg was hid on my bofom——tremblingly

blingly I raised him, and withdrew further.

"Come, Fribourg, let us walk," I
said, "henceforward to myself alone
must I trust for safety. Fribourg is still
more weak than I am; still less than me
can he command his feelings."

"Forbear, Cazire," he replied, look-
ing mournfully upon me, "is it then
nothing to converse, to walk every evening with her my soul adores, and never
till this hour have presumed a kiss upon
her lips? You know not how I have
commanded my feelings—how at this
moment I still hold them in struggling
subjection—how often when my full
heart has ached to madness, have I still
represt

repreſs the keenneſs of its emotions, ſtill
buried deep in my boſom its confuſed
ſenſations, leſt, ungenerous reprover, I
ſhould alarm the ſcrupulous delicacy of
your ideas, leſt I ſhould be unable to
reſume the reins if once I relaxed my
graſp; but now the ſtruggle is over—
I can bear it no longer; this evening
I had intended to confeſs my weakneſs,
you have anticipated me. I can continue thus no more. I over-rated my
own fortitude, my forbearance, when I
demanded your converſe, your ſociety.
Oh, Cazire," he continued, ſinking on
his knees and embracing mine, while his
love fraught eyes were raiſed to my
countenance, " conſent to grant me
that ſociety ſo dear, ſo prized for ever;
fly with me where the world ſhall never
find

find us more, beyond those mountains, beyond the precincts of inhabited nature, to the remotest defert of circling creation, you would form my happiness in the wildeft care; without you I am wretched, without you folitary in the bosom of fociety; fpeak, Cazire, determine; your fiat reprieves me from, or condemns me to————."

" Fribourg," I interrupted, trembling, " do I hear aright? this from you! Your wife, your family, have you forgotten all?"

" No, I remember them well; if you refuse me, henceforward they become as blank in my eftimation—I know them not—"

" Defperate,

" Defperate, cruel man, what would you do?"

" 'Fly them for ever, and wander defolate through the world; your refufal avails them nothing, your compliance may."

" What but mifery to them could my compliance avail? Oh, no, Fribourg, you play upon my feelings you cannot mean as you fay."

" Do not diftract me thus," he cried, " I cannot live without you; why would you continually urge the victory of felf over happinefs?"

" Would you have me plunge head-
long

long in a sea of vice, pursue a deliberate system of the blackest guilt, at once over-turn the only pleasure of which is left me—that of not injuring another?"

" You have already done all the injury you can—acquired the preference of my affection; not to return it now to its fullest extent, would be but adding to your fancied guilt a real injury—that of destroying me."

" Cruel Fribourg, is this my reward? but no matter, you shall not render me guilty as you are unjust."

" Guilty," he returned with a dis-dainful smile; " what would you infer from the term GUILTY?"

" The

" The subverfion of a moral fyftem,"
I returned.

" Of what-moral fyftem?"

" That of marriage, for inftance,"
faid I, " which entails on its innovator
the blackeft guilt; it is a facred inftitu-
tion, the cement of fociety, the parent of
affinity, and all its tender claims; the
incendiary who would deftroy one link
of a chain fo fine, is a traitor to fociety
and an enemy to mankind."

" And to blot an individval from the
face of mirthful day, to deftroy at one
blow the fine-wrought wonders of the
human frame, is nothing in the fcale."

" Fribourg

" Fribourg calls himself a philosopher, and yet knows not the first article
of his creed—Fortitude in the endur-
ance of evil."

" Evils which cannot be remedied,"
he resumed. " Philosophy dictates
perseverance when they can."

" But when the remedy is more desperate than the evil, Fribourg——"

" We shall always find cold-hearted
calculators enough to draw us back, to
point at distant joys with the wan finger
of suspicion, and bid us explore away
our lives in doubt ere we attempt to
certify. Cazire, be not always the prudential moralizer; you yield enough
to

to the prejudices of the world, yield somewhat to nature, to the heart."

" Well, Fribourg," I replied, as I felt my love struggling with my reason, as though determined upon victory, " give me but this night to resolve; grant me," I falteringly added, " grant me a respite from myself."

" Be it so, and to-morrow then—"

" To-morrow you shall have my answer—now farewell."

" I resign you, Cazire—I pursue no farther the faint dawnings of acquiescence; let my forbearance teach you mercy."

So faying he fuffered my departure;
it was neceffary I fhould pafs his houfe
to reach my brother's; I could not forbear ftealing a confcious glance at the
windows; the fhutters of that which
fronted the road, and which were low
enough to admit obfervation of what was
paffing in the room, were only partially
clofed; the light which fhone through
the opening tempted me nearer; I approached, and beheid the wife of Fribourg
feated in a melancholy attitude by the
fire, her cheek refted on her hand, and
an open volume laid on the table before
her; two children were playing on the
floor, and methought the grief which
preyed upon her mind diftracted her
attention from the book; doubtlefs
fhe lamented the continual defertion
of

of her hufband, and deprecated me as
the caufe; and yet, no—her countenance was all that refignation could
pourtray, a melancholy langour over-
fpread her penfive features, but there
was no expreffion of anger or defpair;
one fhould have thought from her looks
the deftroying paffions of mankind were
ftrangers to her breaft; a fanctified forrow and holy meeknefs, which it were a
crime to outrage, feemed alone to reign
there.

Never before had I felt fo keenly the
deep humiliation of guilt; how different did I feel myfelf to this injured,
wretched woman; it was I who caufed
that look of deeply hidden forrow—it
was I who barbed with agony the mor-

K 2   tifying

tifying fhaft of fcorn that rankled in her patient breaft—, was I who taught an hufband's hand to hurl the cruel dart; yet fhe, poor innocent, had never injured me, but, lurking in ambufh, I was her bittereft, her rankeft foe; in fecret I wove a wreath of thorns to lacerate her chaftened brow; wretched monfter that I felt myfelf, how durft I live, and know that an all-feeing eye contemplated her and me at once!

I was on the point of rufhing into her prefence and confeffing all my guilt, of fwearing never more to fee her hufband, of abjuring for ever at her feet my fatal paffion; in her keen reproaches I fhould half expiate my crime; by future repentance

pentance perhaps blot it from the book
of the recording angel.

Suddenly I felt myself haſtily drawn
back; I turned—'twas Fribourg.

" Raſh, romantic girl," he cried,
" what do you here?"

My heart was too full to anſwer; I
ſuffered him to lead me from the gate;
and, a prey to the keeneſt emotions,
returned home.

CHAP. XVI.

THE TRIUMPH.

THAT my agitation might not be remarked, I walked into the garden, hoping the air would recover me; it was separated at the end by a flight fence from an adjoining field, and I approached some flower pots as though I intended to remove them; after displacing several, scarcely conscious of what I was doing, I discovered beneath one a letter; immediately

mediately I remembered what my
unknown correspondent had faid, I made
no doubt but the letter was from him,
which chance had indeed directed me
to it: I placed it in my bofom, and
when I retired to my chamber, read as
follows:

"Miferable girl! if yet a fpark of
virtue glimmers in your benighted bofom
forbear your prefent conduct; with grief
and horror, but not furprife, I view your
growing intimacy with the dangerous
Fribourg; he is a free thinker and an
atheift: your only chance of fafety is
to fly him; in vain would you addrefs
his fceptic foul in the language of virtue; nothing with him is virtue but the
gratification of his boundlefs paffions;

he

he acknowledges no God but pleasure, and therefore fears no punishment—religion is a farce with him, therefore can he never feel compunction; he believes in no law, divine or human, therefore never imagines he can break any; the avenue to his sophisticated heart is guarded with the strength of hell—like a pestilential vault, in seeking to purify it you will yourself become infected—and to seek his reformation is a task so dangerous, it will entail your own seduction.

" 1 feel it my duty to warn you, for yet it may not be too late; you stand upon the verge of a precipice; while yet you can shrink back, there is more merit, Cazire, suddenly to stop in the

path

path of deſtruction than never to have entered it.

"Beware, I entreat you, the dangerous ſophiſms of this man; he acts upon a ſyſtem of his own—be his convert, and you inevitably become his victim. Reaſon with yourſelf awhile, unbiaſſed by the falſe alluring viſions of a madman; let not his ſpecious arguments ſtifle the conſcious whiſperings of inſulted virtue; for, believe me, where there is no guilt, we feel no doubt—we ſeek not by refinement to reconcile that which reaſon already approves.

"ARIEL."

Softened

Softened as I was, this letter deeply imprest my spirits; already I saw myself half sunk in vice—I almost feared that struggling would not save me; it was evident my unknown advifer knew my frequent meetings with Fribourg—evident too he dreaded the interest he was daily gaining over me, and abhorred the singular freedom of his tenets; but the stranger had said, he saw my conduct with horror, not surprise. Had I ever given proofs then of future depravity?—was he acquainted with the wild effervescence of my sentiments?—and was the height of romantic enthusiasm nearly allied to vice? Alas! I have since learnt that stability of principle and confiftency of idea not liable to be shaken

by

by the dangerous gales of fophiftry, are
the fureft foundations of virtue

It was yet midnight, and thoughtfully
I ruminated on my conduct; methought
till now I had been hurrying onwards to
an abyfs of guilt; I determined to make
a laft effort to roufe, as it were, my dor-
mant faculties to ftruggle againft the
delufions of paffion, and fee Fribourg no
more.

Scarcely had I refolved on this, when
I fancied him before me, trembling,
anxious for the fuccefs of his love, liftening with panting hope for my decifion !
overwhelmed, defpairing as with agonized reluctance, I pronounced my duty.

" No,

" No, never can I execute the tafk,"
I exclaimed, ftarting from the fide of my
bed ; " no, if it is a crime to love, that
crime is paft ; I will fly with him then
to fome remote defart, together we will
pafs the few fhort hours of exiftence ; it
is folly thus to ftruggle againft the heart
—together we will tread at dawn the
flower-befprinkled mead, feek out from
their fad abode the gloomy children of
forrow, and fill their hearts with renovated hope. Yes, yes, by the virtue of
our future actions will we obtain for-
givenefs for a fingle crime."

But I had no fooner ended my rhap-
fody, when before the buoyant eye of
fancy flitted the pale fhadows of Fribourg's wife and children; menacing at

me

me they pointed; I pierced into their
gloomy retreat; together I faw them
mourn the defertion of a father and an
hufband; dim and cold feemed their
cheerlefs habitation—the ftillnefs of
death appeared to reign among them;
fhuddering I withdrew my vifionary
gaze, and covered my face with my
hands.

" Oh, heaven affift me to decide," I
faid, " inftruct me how to act; oh!
Fribourg, could I but guide thy wandering judgment, reform thy apoftate fentiments; once convinced by the divine
truth of virtue, Fribourg would fave me
from myfelf. I will write to him; but
Ariel had faid, to attempt his reformation

tion was to entail my own feduction. Well then, Fribourg is noble, is capable of heroic magnanimity when he believes himfelf inftigated by duty; yes, I will write to him, and, confcious of my weaknefs, throw myfelf upon his mercy for protection.

At length by dawn, after deftroying feveral letters, I produced the following:

" I am going, Fribourg, to folicit your compaffion; oppofe not my weaknefs with your ftrength, but lend your arm to flay me.

" 'Tis

" 'Tis in vain I would believe that yielding the reins to inclination is criminal only in the eyes of prejudice ; if fo, whence the confufion of my prefent fenfations ?—whence the palpitation of my doubting heart ?—whence the chill horror which bedews my brow ?—how, if I am actuated by prejudice alone, do I feel, when refolving to yield all to love, a fentiment of guilt, till then unknown ? —how, if withheld by prejudice alone, does a determination to abide by it, footh at once my mental perturbation, cool the glowing anguifh of my agitated bofom ? Surely the power that can caufe emotions fo varied, fo widely different from each other as anarchy and peace, muft be fomething more than prejudice ; or, allowing it were not, ftill

entering

entering so firmly in the heart, ought it with dangerous violence to be rooted thence?

"I feel that to resign myself to you, to abide by the dictates of my love alone would yield me; why should I not acknowledge it, for that at least may be allowed; joy inexpressible! never to miss you from my side, to reason with you on the fallacy of your principles; and, oh, rapture! instead of becoming your convert, to render you mine; this would indeed be to me the climax of earthly happiness; but it would be an happiness which I dare not indulge, the hopes of which I dare not even believe; like the glow-worm which shines brightly in the night, at dawn of day it fades; it

is

is a pleasing dream that vanishes as I awake, that essaying to sleep would again recall; when a child I have closed my eyes upon the light, and fancied visions of such dazzling splendor, that methought to open them again and destroy my fairy fabric were a pain.

" I almost wish, Fribourg, that I could think as you do; but to act in direct opposition to my ideas of right would in me at least be guilt; place yourself in my situation; if you thought your love for me a crime, would you nor struggle against it?—would you still urge me to return it? No—for true love never yet sought the degradation of its object. Convince, if you can, my reason in addition to my feelings; convince

vince me that to fhudder at deftroying
the peace of a family is prejudice ; convince me if you can that it is an imaginary crime to ftab the bofom of a wife,
and ruin the early profpect of her
children ; tell me that the world is all a
cheat, that pain and pleafure are the
diftinctions of an hypochondriac, that
vice and virtue are but the terms of folly
or the tools of knaves ; tell me that the
univerfe is an ample pleafure garden,
formed alike for the recreation of all ;
or, tell me' rather it is a barbarous wil-
dernefs, whence civilization is exploded,
and the tumultuous favage revels at large
as fancy dictates, or as defire excites ;
fay that man is at liberty to purfue his
prey through the panting heart of his
neighbour, if there it could take refuge

and

and fay at once that univerfal anarchy is the law of nature.

" Fribourg, can that be real happi-nefs which fhrinks from the analyfis of truth?—the fuperior fentiment I expe-rience when I refolve to conquer my wifhes—when I think that not for me fhall the pillow of your wife be fteeped in tears, nor the afcending curfes of your children reach to heaven; oh! then I feel that the deepeft fenfation of mifery is luxury when compared to confcious guilt.

" Fribourg, let us endeavour to con-quer the fatality of our paffion, let us not purfue it to the gates of deftruction,

to

to forbear to love may be an useless
attempt; to love, yet forbear to gratify
it, may be noble; humanity, as near as
possible, reaches perfection, when in
mercy to others it disclaims the preference of self.

"Tell me, Fribourg, that I am right,
that we may love without guilt, that it
even becomes a virtue when we with-
stand its seductions.

"CAZIRE ARIENI."

After I had written this, still dissatis-
fied, still fearing I had not energetically
enough expressed to Fribourg my sensations;

lations; I threw myself upon the bed,
and endeavouring to rejoice in my painful victory, fought in fleep a temporary
forgetfulnefs.

CHAP. XVII.

THE RELAPSE.

ON awaking I flew immediately to the window—Fribourg was walking in the garden—I foftly called him, and he raifed his eyes.

" I have been walking here thefe two hours," he faid in a reproachful accent.

I defcended; I approached the rail-ings,

ings, and placing my letter in his hand, retired with precipitancy.

Towards evening I again fought the garden; Fribourg was already there; I received from him a letter; he trembled with agitation as he gave it me, and then retired as I had done.

I read thus:

" Confidence is the only bafis on which affection builds its towering pyramid; doubt is the damp which moulders it away—it is the canker-worm that never dies; like the fair rofe, inly infefted by a fecret foe, ftill its bright leaves retain their hue; ftill to the outward

ward eye looks fair even at the moment in which it falls; but, Cazire, the heart is deſtroyed.

" Could I be content with ſuch a fancied Eden? could I revel in your ſmiles, and know the ſtorm within, doubt deſtroying doubt, which grows by what it feeds on, and views with microſcopic eye all earthly joy, making in the end that real, which appeared ſo?—confidence in yourſelf, Cazire; confidence un-bounded, can be alone unbounded affec-tion: yours is ſhackled, is deſtroyed by the fetters of prejudice.

" Love is like a beauteous bird; it ſeeks to neſtle in your boſom, you place a chain of iron upon its downy wing, you

you affix a boundary to its soft approach
✳ ✳ ✳ ✳ ✳ ✳ ✳ ✳ ✳ ✳ ✳ ✳
✳ ✳ ✳ ✳ ✳ ✳ ✳ ✳ ✳ ✳ ✳ ✳
✳ ✳ ✳ ✳ ✳ ✳ ✳ ✳ ✳ ✳ ✳

"In the romance of my earliest youth
I have contracted friendships with those
who seemed congenial to me: perhaps
at the time they were sincere; but interest, circumstance, predicament, step-
ped in between them and their friendship—they deserted me, they grieved
me—but I scorned to pursue them; I
looked round upon the aggregate of
society, I found them ready at all times
to laugh away the hours of existence,
but I sought a friend who could improve,
or bid them pass in rational delight;

my

my heart shrunk with apathy from the
coldnefs of worldly connections, and,
wrapped in its filent forrow, lamented
the infenfibility of man.

"At length I married; it was a ftep
of defperation, and failed of yielding me
the folace I expected; it fmoothed not
in its placid, even chain the effervefcence of my foul, and again I felt
myfelf condemned to feek in fociety
that fympathy I could not find in the
bofom of my family; yet there too
was I ftill difappointed, difgufted, and
left an ifolated being on the face of ani-
mated nature.

"The gradual decay of hope filled
me

me with gloomy mifanthropy; the re-
fources I poffeffed in mylelf became
my only confolation; in philofophic
feclufion I indulged them, yet were
they not fufficiently ftrong to ftifle the
longings of an ardent and fufceptible
heart for loving a beloved object; need
I fay I found in you the latter?—you
have fince acknowledged the former; I
imbibed for you an unbounded and ex-
quifite attachment—you gave me hope,
you bade it arife from the afhes of
defpair, bade it bloom over its tomb,
yet now again all is crufhed, and
again I fhut my lattice on the
world.

" All I have experienced fickens my

foul

foul with forrow: I fhall turn ftoic,
and view mankind as from an eminence.

"Methought the injuftice I had fuf-
tained in my intercourfe with fociety
was fufficient; I did not believe that
Cazire, who had fo nearly filled my
exhaufted cup with fupreme felicity,
would fuddenly dafh it to the earth ere
my parched lips had tafted; this indeed
was giving the climax to my difappoint-
ments.

"I fhall not, however, attempt to
combat your arguments: you are a flave
to prejudice, but they are prejudices
which make your happinefs; and fo
long

long as we are happy, Cazire, it does not
matter how; you was formed for a ge-
nuine child of nature ; you would have
been fo, but the tide of cuftom has
proved too ftrong—it tinctures our ideas
with its gloomy influence, it becomes
incorporated with our actions, our
thoughts; you have been fuffered to
run wild, yet have learnt prudence—
prejudice I would fay, in the very lap
of folitude; but remember, Cazire, that
real life, and life depicted in romance,
are widely different; through all its
variations, the former feldom concludes
happily; the latter is twifted from the
breaft of probability; events are made
fubfervient, and the falfe imagery ends
in a delufive peace; romances corrupt

the

the imagination, and fill it with visions of chaotic inconsistencies.

" The die however is now cast; happiness is of a texture too fine to bear anatomising, and I must seek no further to influence you.

" I never before imagined it my duty to relinquish you; now I begin to perceive that were I even successful in revolutionising your sentiments, I should only render you miserable; at this idea my heart chills; you never would be firmly established in the justice of your own conduct—a corroding fear would prey upon your every pleasure; oh! not to purchase to myself the joy of your exclusive

clusive possession, of your dear society,
would I gaze upon the care-worn traces
of your cheek, hear your despondent
struggling sigh, or haunt your soul with
the dread vision of a future curse.

"I resign then my happiness to yours;
for you I would forego my soul, my life,
my all; 'twould be a crime too great to
convince your reason, unless, by doing
so, I could for ever exterminate your
doubts; age would creep on, the enthusiasm which might temporarily gild your
conversion, the warm tide of youthful
passion which might spread a charm over
your fancied apostacy, must gradually
subside, the evening of your days would
close in gloom, and the wretched Fri-

bourg

L 4

bourg would receive the dying curfe of Cazire.

Thus far have I painfully brought myfelf, ever fwayed by that which I conceive my duty, unbiaffed, 'tis true, by what the world denominates fuch. I relinquifh you, Cazire, relinquifh you and feel as though I tore the heart from my bofom to fave it from a future ftab. One thing only I require; I have yielded to the dreadful impulfe of juftice but I can do no more—I cannot wield with fmiles its fiery torch, and gaze upon the havoc it has caufed; I dare not truft myfelf amid your fyren fafcinations, left I be tempted to curfe my hard wrung neceffary facrifice; I can fee you

no

no more—voluntarily I have figned my own condemnation; Cazire's mercy will preferve me from the rack.

"AUGUSTUS FRIBOURG."

———

With what varied fenfations did I perufe this letter; how did I lament, admire, and adore the noble heroifm of my beloved Fribourg; how, with invincible anguifh, did I gaze upon the words, "I relinquifh you, Cazire;" how did I yet reverence him for his noble refignation of an heart that long had been his own; deeper than ever now reigned his image in my
L 5   bofom.

bofom. Surely I had been too precipitate—duty, juftice, never could require fuch a facrifice; I had trampled on a love the moft ardent—I now faw the moft difintere{ted, the moft generous; how, at any future period of exiftence, could ever I make him or myfelf amends?—I had ftabbed him to his bofom's core, yet, without a murmur, did he bear the lacerated wound.

"But," whifpered felf-love, "would Fribourg, could he debar himfelf from feeing me?—would he abide by the magnanimity of his refolve? I fhould have wifhed him to poflefs the power, but I was not fufficiently philofophic. Vanity made me hope, imprudent as I felt

felt it, that again he had over-rated his
fortitude; variable and inconstant being
that I was, the creature of passion and
the moment; continually aware of what
virtue required, tremblingly alive to its
slightest deviations, yet without fortitude
to abide by its decisions, without even
firmness at all times to desire it.

All day was I employed near the
window, watching for the entrance of
Fribourg to triumph in the weakness I
should have deplored, (which a moment
before I had been endeavouring to arm)
and see reviving, like the phœnix
from its ashes, the ascendancy I had
gained over him; evening however
came—night approached, and yet no

signs

figns of Fribourg. Difcontented, angry
with myfelf, and almoft doubting his
love, I retired defpondent to my room,
but I flept not during the night; at
dawn again I was at the window, again I
glowed with hope, again my blood fer-
mented with the agitation of my mind;
the fun gained its meridian, declined in
the weft; he came not; pride only
faved me from entering the garden; he
defpifed me furely for the eafinefs of
my love, for the franknefs with which I
had acknowledged it; his wife had regained her juft empire over his mind—
the empire I had refigned; or, perhaps,
he fought a kinder, a lefs fcrupulous
heart than mine—madnefs!—had then
the ftruggles of my foul, in refigning

him,

him, availed nothing to his wife?—was it
for another, a wretch, probably, whofe
only merit would confift in returning the
ardor of his love, that I had given up
the joy of my foul? Miferable tor-
mentor!—no! If the love of Fribourg
was fo eafy of transfer, it muft be worth-
lefs; and yet to make no effort, no
more endeavour to attach me to him, to
influence my decifion, fo readily at once
to refign all! he could not have loved
me ever—human nature was incapable
of fuch fudden, fuch immediate victory;
'twas folly, 'twas madnefs to believe he
had ever loved; and yet, heaven! perhaps Fribourg was ill, or wandering in
fome gloomy wild a prey to defpondency
and woe; perhaps reclining on the earth,
he

he lamented the heedlefs capture of his heart—perhaps no fleep had vifited his eyes.

" Oh, Fribourg, Fribourg," I exclaimed, " where art thou? let me retract all—let me ftill be thine."

Evening fpread around her many-coloured mantle—night clofed on my woes —I felt it impoffible to exift another day in fuch refined torture; an intenfe fever fwelled in my veins, my heart beat agonizing rapidity, and a wild, irregular pulfation betrayed the derangement of my bodily, as well as mental fyftem.

At the firft ftreak of dawn I arofe with an

an heavy figh—it was the third morning
that I had not feen my Fribourg; was
it poffible he had exifted fo long without
me?—that I ftill breathed debarred of his
fociety; how great a charm did it leave
in my exiftence—I felt how dear he was
to my foul; no more I endeavoured to
conquer the fatality of my paffion—I
believed it a vain attempt; the day paft
on, I faw him not; in a diftraction of
mind, impoffible to be depicted, fcarcely
confcious how I began or finifhed, I
wrote a few lines, while my eyes failed
to identify the traces of my trembling
pen.

" I feel myfelf incapable longer of
                                    fupporting

supporting your abfence: if ever you
loved, if you even wifh me to retain my
faculties entire, come, I befeech you,
into the garden; I am no more the
implacable judge, refining on your torture—you fhall be judge, and hold my
fiat in your hands; hope what you will,
I can ftruggle no longer againft the
overwhelming tide.

" CAZIRE."

Pride faved me no farther; its whifperings were difregarded, and as the dews
of evening defcended, I entered the
garden. Half an hour had elapfed;
prefently I perceived the little fon of
Fribourg.

Fribourg, who, as ufual, poor innocent, flew towards me; where was the delicacy of my virtue flown, where its former fufceptibility, where the purity of my intentions, when I could make the unconfcious child, who had before affected me with fuch lively tranfports of remorfe and forrow, the conductor of a letter to his father?—all, all fwallowed up in the devouring fever of an ungovernable paffion. My hand fhook as I gave it into his, I blufhed the dye of fcarlet; and a fingle fcalding tear, which evinced my compunction and my weaknefs, fell upon his innocent countenance as he raifed it for a kifs.

" Go," I faid in a voice almoft inarticulate

articulate from emotion, " and give that
to your father."

He flew to obey me, but I could no
longer fupport the humiliating reflection
of my own guilt, I cold no longer fupport the light of Heaven, the ferene
majefty of its unclouded expanfe, and
flew with agony from the fpot.

END OF THE FIRST VOLUME.

PRINTED BY D. N. SHURY, BERWICK-STREET, SOHO.

GOTHIC NOVELS

ARNO PRESS

in cooperation with

McGrath Publishing Company

Dacre, Charlotte ("Rosa Matilda"). **Confessions of the Nun of St. Omer,** A Tale. 2 vols. 1805. New Introduction by Devendra P. Varma.

Godwin, William. **St. Leon:** A Tale of the Sixteenth Century. 1831. New Foreword by Devendra P. Varma. New Introduction by Juliet Beckett.

Lee, Sophia. **The Recess:** Or, A Tale of Other Times. 3 vols. 1783. New Foreword by J. M. S. Tompkins. New Introduction by Devendra P. Varma.

Lewis, M[atthew] G[regory], trans. **The Bravo of Venice,** A Romance. 1805. New Introduction by Devendra P. Varma.

Prest, Thomas Preskett. **Varney the Vampire.** 3 vols. 1847. New Foreword by Robert Bloch. New Introduction by Devendra P. Varma.

Radcliffe, Ann. **The Castles of Athlin and Dunbayne:** A Highland Story. 1821. New Foreword by Frederick Shroyer.

Radcliffe, Ann. **Gaston De Blondeville.** 2 vols. 1826. New Introduction by Devendra P. Varma.

Radcliffe, Ann. **A Sicilian Romance.** 1821. New Foreword by Howard Mumford Jones. New Introduction by Devendra P. Varma.

Radcliffe, Mary-Anne. **Manfroné:** Or The One-Handed Monk. 2 vols. 1828. New Foreword by Devendra P. Varma. New Introduction by Coral Ann Howells.

Sleath, Eleanor. **The Nocturnal Minstrel.** 1810. New Introduction by Devendra P. Varma.